CLAIMED

KING BROTHERS BOOK ONE

LISA LANG BLAKENEY

WRITERGIRL PRESS

LISA LANG BLAKENEY
Love reading novels featuring hot alpha men who fall for smart women?
Then join <u>MY VIP MAILING LIST</u> at http://LisaLangBlakeney.com/VIP and
get a **free** book just for joining!

FOLLOW ME
Follow me on Facebook
Join my Fan Group
Follow me on Amazon
Follow me on Bookbub
Follow me on Instagram

LICENSE NOTE

WHAT READERS ARE SAYING
ABOUT LISA

"Lisa writes books that are intense. Explosive. Panty Melting. Raw. Exposed. Angst. Multifaceted."

"Cover to cover, page by page every word was amazing. This author is amazing and her work is even more amazing. She really can get all the details and words to sound great together."

"As soon as I picked up book 1 I was addicted to this series. I couldn't wait for this one to come out!"

"I definitely recommend this series to readers. It was the first of its kind that I have read, and I was not disappointed. 5 Stars!"

This book is dedicated to my friend Deb Carroll.
A woman who fell in love with & tirelessly supports
my characters just as much as I do!

BOOKS BY LISA

The Masterson Series

Devour this addictive series about the possessive bad boy, Roman Masterson, who falls hard and fast for the girl he's promised his family to protect.

Masterson

Masterson Unleashed

Masterson In Love

Masterson Made

Joseph Loves Juliette

The King Brothers Series

Dive into this series of interconnected standalones featuring 3 alpha hot brothers and the women they lay claim to without apology.

Claimed - Camden & Jade

Indebted - Cutter & Sloan

Broken - Stone & Tiny

Promised - All King Brothers

The Nighthawk Series

Sexy & sweet sports romances set in the professional world of football. All standalones.

Saint - Saint & Sabrina

Wolf - Cooper & Ursula

Diesel - Mason & Olivia

Jett - Jett & Adrienne

Rush - Rush & Mia

The Valencia Mafia Series

Coming Soon. Get Notified!

INTRODUCTION

An Alpha Who Claims His Woman Without Apology

"Camden King Is Coming For Me."

I work for him, but I can't stand him.
I slept with him once, and he never lets me forget it.
Camden King thinks he can have me again...and again...and
again. But he can't...I won't let that happen.
I just have to last thirty days to prove it to him.
Will I be able to hold out?
Or have I finally met my match...

PROLOGUE

The Harbor Hotel
Baltimore, Maryland
Three Months Ago

CAMDEN

I'm not a big talker.

I keep to myself.

If someone needs to make a lot of noise, I let my brother Cutter handle that. Cutter often describes me as the silent and deadly type. That may be a somewhat accurate characterization of me, but I like to think of myself as careful instead.

A watcher.

Someone who calculates risk before taking it. Someone who observes a situation long and hard before striking. But when I finally do make the decision to act, I don't fuck around. I handle my business. Which is what brings me here standing in front of the five-star Harbor Hotel of Baltimore, Maryland.

I've run a million scenarios in my head.
I've calculated the risk.
And I think it's fucking worth it.
Tonight … I'm taking what's mine.
I've been patient long enough.

JADE

The Harbor Hotel
Baltimore, Maryland
Three Months Ago

I'm in the bathroom, in my birthday suit, contemplating the day I've just had. As I sip on my second large cocktail consisting of Grey Goose vodka and pineapple juice over ice, I finish wiping off the remnants of my so-called waterproof mascara, and start running the tub when I hear a knock at my hotel room door.

I'm feeling no pain, but the knock is loud enough that I hear it over my old school nineties jams streaming through an app on my phone. I don't think anything of the interruption, though, because I'm expecting an overpriced Cobb salad and an iced tea from room service. So I wrap the oversized bath sheet around my nude body, run to the door, crack it open to let the server in, and immediately turn back to attend to my tub full of water.

"You can just leave the platter on the bed," I call out. Running back to the bubbles and cocktail waiting for me.

But it isn't anyone from room service. It's a greeting from a deep, rolling, familiar voice that makes my stomach flip and flutter instead.

"Where are you running off to, itty bitty?"

I whip my head around in shock. Strands of my hair flying in my mouth. Only one person calls me that particular nickname, and he has no business being here.

"What the hell?!" The words tumble out of my mouth.

"Come again?"

The *voice* doesn't like it when I curse at him. Never mind the fact that he has a foul mouth too. Never mind the fact that he is here invading *my* space, not the other way around, so in my opinion a couple of curse words are definitely called for.

"Let me speak clearer for you then." I make sure to enunciate all my consonants and vowels. Especially the bad ones. "What the *hell* are you doing in my hotel room? No wait, what the *fuck* are you doing in Maryland, period?"

"Handling some business, and watch your fucking mouth."

My boss Camden King, deliciously dressed in all black, steps completely into my room, lets the door click shut, and carefully drops his signature black leather backpack on the floor. As soon as I hear the thump of his bag hitting the carpeted entryway, the room suddenly becomes several square feet smaller.

I can barely breathe.

His cocky dominance takes up so much oxygen, and there's a seriousness etched across his beautifully chiseled face that frightens and fascinates me at the same time.

"What business?" I ask with a faux confidence. Not even realizing that I am walking backwards towards the wall as he moves silently forward like the predator that he is quickly revealing himself to be.

I stop moving when I can't any longer, my back finally against the wall, white knuckling the corners of my towel, making sure that it stays closed. Because if it slips even just a little, I think I will end up slipping.

Slipping right on top of his enormous dick.

I hate to admit it to myself, but *doing* Camden King has been a reoccurring theme in many of my dreams lately. Dreams I hoped would cease very soon, because they are a pain in my ass and a strain on my vibrator. Not to mention that I couldn't or wouldn't ever make the decision to *actually* fuck my boss.

Only in my dreams.

Or so I keep telling myself.

The two of us stare at each other for a moment in uneasy silence. We don't really need words at the moment, because the fact that he is here speaks volumes. Camden doesn't travel much outside of the Philadelphia area. Not unless it's absolutely required for a job, and being in Baltimore was certainly not a job requirement. We don't have any clients in the area, and we both are actually supposed to be somewhere else tonight.

The beauty of my relationship with my employers: Camden, Cutter and Roman has always been that it's a simple and straight forward relationship. I work for them. They pay me. I take care of them. They protect me. But we give each other a wide berth when it comes to our private lives. They have their women. Lots of women. And I've had my dalliances too, but no one interferes in each other's lives.

At least not until today.

"What are you doing in this hotel, Jade?" he asks while closing the gap between us even more. "Why aren't you home attending the fundraiser?"

There was an important autism fundraising event hosted by Roman's stepmother that we both were supposed to

5

attend. I was planning all week to be there, but decided at the last minute to come here instead. I didn't tell anyone where I was going, because there would have been too many questions. Questions I wasn't ready to answer.

"Why aren't *you* there?" I counter.

"I asked first," he says while flashing that very wicked smile of his.

"What business is it of yours?"

"Last time I checked you are my business." He takes a long pause for effect then finishes his thought. "You work for me, remember?"

"Well if you want to get technical about things, Roman is the one who hired me."

"I think you're very confused." Camden practically growls in my face.

At this point, we are standing so close to each other that I feel drenched in his scent. All of the domineering men I work for have a signature aroma, but Camden always smells the best. Earthy and natural. Like he sweats sandalwood and leather. The scent is utterly intoxicating and must be permanently etched in my olfactory senses, because sometimes I wake up in the morning and swear that I can actually smell him in my apartment. Which is completely impossible, because Camden has never been inside of my place, and Lord knows that I'm trying to keep it that way.

"You answer to three men. Roman, me, and my brother. Of course tonight you have the distinct pleasure of only having to answer to me," he says while running the backs of his fingers gingerly down the side of my face. The unexpected touch of his calloused knuckles almost takes my breath away. *What is he doing?*

"Listen, Camden—"

"No, you listen."

He's so close that his lips are actually touching mine as he continues to speak. His eyes almost dancing. "I tracked you, I followed you, and I'm not leaving until I get what I came for."

He firmly grabs me around my waist with one hand, and places his other on the hand that is holding my towel in place.

"What did you—"

He cuts off my idiotic question with his mouth, and kisses me like he was trying to teach me a lesson. A lesson on how to fuck someone's mouth properly. A lesson on how to shut a woman up in the most pleasurable way possible. A lesson on never questioning why Camden does anything he does. It would be pointless. Especially if he was going to do shit like this to stop me.

I haven't allowed myself to completely let go though. I'm still highly strung like a tightly wound clock, because I haven't been kissed like this since … well I've never been kissed like this. I've only had one serious relationship in my life, which was a complete disaster from start to finish, and then a string of meaningless fucks afterwards.

I never kiss them.

It's one of my rules.

A rule I seem to have completely thrown to the wayside as Camden's tongue expertly and languidly explores mine. Soft, tender, exploratory strokes of his tongue that are loosening me up with each swipe. His skills are so amazing that they make me wonder just how good it would feel if he used them on other areas of my body.

Probably would be life changing.

There's no way I can let things get to that point though, because that would be damn near close to breaking my *never going to fuck my boss* rule. Unfortunately Camden's expert command of my mouth and my inability to respond appropriately because of it starts to shake my resolve.

I release the taut hold I had on my towel. Then he lifts his hand away from mine and slides it in my hair at the nape of my neck.

Cradling the back and side of my head.

Stroking his thumb gently near the corner of my mouth.

Pulling me farther into him.

Deepening our kiss.

And ratcheting up the heat factor.

I completely let go of the towel. It feels stupid to keep holding onto it in the middle of us passionately making out, because that is indeed what we are doing, even though my hands are still in between us. Serving as the last remaining barrier between the two of us making full bodily contact.

I can't place my arms around his neck like I want to, because Camden is so much taller than me, so I slide them around his waist instead. Decision made. If this is going to happen, then it's going to happen. Maybe it was meant to be. There's no one here to interrupt us. There's no one to talk me out of it. There's just me and him. No one will have to know. It could be a one time thing. Another meaningless fuck. It would have to be.

He's my boss and someone I've known for a long time, and because of those two things, he knows entirely too much about me, and I know quite a bit about him as well. Things that would make going beyond one night complicated and awkward. So yeah, it could never be more than one night in this hotel room for both of our sakes.

Camden abruptly pulls away from the kiss and glares at me almost angrily. As if he's upset that he's just kissed me, or something. *Me too, buddy,* I think to myself. I never thought I would be kissing Camden King naked in a hotel room.

Honestly, I have no idea what he's thinking. Which is one of the things that drives me absolutely nuts about Camden. I can't read his facial expressions or lack thereof for shit. Which makes handling him that much more of a challenge.

It's always been like that, and oddly enough, one of the things that draws me to him.

"What?" I ask open-mouthed.

He slowly rakes his eyes up and down my nude body before asking the craziest question.

"Are you fucking someone here?"

"What?!"

"Did I stutter? I asked you if you're fucking someone."

"What does that matter?"

"Not the right answer, Jade."

"Don't make this more difficult."

"Don't make *what* more difficult?"

"Whatever I think is about to happen in this room."

"Nothing is going to happen in this room until you tell me if you're fucking someone or not."

"Are you actually trying to throw down an ultimatum? Let's not forget that I didn't invite you here. You barged your way in here. I could care less whether anything happens between us tonight or not."

"Your pussy begs to differ."

"You don't know shit about what's in between my legs, and you never will."

I bend down to pick up my towel, suddenly very self-conscious about my lack of clothing.

"Anyone who stepped inside of this room right now would know. You can smell it. It's wet. It's weeping. It's hungry. And I made it that way."

For just a moment his gifted kissing technique made me forget what an arrogant prick Camden King can be, and the reason why I in fact have rules in place to begin with.

"Get out," I order firmly.

"I'm not going any motherfucking where," he growls.

"I don't want you here. Get out—"

He cuts my words off again, but this time with one of his

hands wrapped around my throat and the other shoved between my legs. I inadvertently drop the towel again, and immediately feel a warm gush between my legs as he slides his fingers back and forth between my folds.

Assertively and expertly.

My knees would have buckled if it weren't for the fact that he was firmly holding me against the wall by my neck. I am so turned on by his passionate manhandling of me, I can't think straight and the yeses seem to keep flying out of my mouth.

"Do you like how this feels, Jade?"

"Yes," I moan like the weakling the vodka has made me.

"Do you want me to keep doing this until you come on my hand?"

Dammit, he's dirty too.

"Yes," I exhale in defeat.

"So are you going to be a good girl and answer my question?" His deep voice rumbles closely beside my ear as he continues to stroke me between my legs.

"Yes," I gasp in pleasure.

"Yes you *are* fucking someone here?"

His hand stops moving.

"No," I puff out in frustration. Sick of the twenty questions. "The only person I'm fucking is you in about three seconds in this hotel room."

"Good fucking answer, itty bitty."

JADE

I'm totally mind fucked. The second after I give Camden the answer he wants to hear his hands instantly drop down and away from me. I can't believe how my body immediately misses his confident grasp, the slight pressure around my neck, and the way he was stroking me. Somehow without prior knowledge, this big pain in my ass knows exactly what my body likes and what it needs, and God help me, but I'm desperately craving more.

"Pick up the towel you dropped and spread it on the bed. I don't care how nice of a hotel this is, hotel bed spreads are gross."

I do what he asks as he starts taking off his jacket, but there is something about touching the towel again that triggers my memory. The water.

"Shit!" I scream as I take off flying towards the bathroom. "I left the tub running."

Sure enough there is the beginning of a major flood in the beautiful marbled bathroom of my five-star hotel room. Well more than just the beginnings. The floor is damn near completely covered in water, and I know I'll have to pay a mint if I don't quickly figure out a way to sop it all up.

While I'm wading my feet in flood water, wondering what the heck I am going to do, Camden runs out into the hallway, locates a housekeeping cart, and swipes a stack of towels. Next thing I know, we both are on all fours, mopping up water with white fluffy towels, when room service knocks. I'm actually still naked as a jaybird, so Camden does the honor of answering the door.

"It better be fucking room service for one," he says in an accusatory tone. Still obviously suspicious that I am in Baltimore to meet a man.

"Oh be quiet and get the door," I fuss back.

I hear Camden answer the door, mumble a few words, then close it; but when he never comes back into the bathroom, I get a little nervous. After finishing up wiping the last of the water, I go back out into the suite's main area to see what he's up to, and find that he has made himself quite comfortable.

The lights have been dimmed, the bedspread taken off, and the sheets of the bed are pulled down. He's taken off his black motorcycle boots, his shirt, and leather jacket. And all he is wearing are his black cargo pants, a leather cuff on his wrist, and a sexy smirk across his face.

I should be annoyed. He's being so ridiculously presumptuous. I mean have I ever given him reason to think that I'd be down for this? But it's difficult to be genuinely miffed about his impromptu visit when I'm practically drooling over the jerk right now.

He looks amazing.

Downright delicious.

I've always known that Camden takes care of himself. He eats well, works out, and I've definitely seen him without a shirt on over the years, but getting a full on view of his diamond cut six-pack in soft bedroom lighting, with that hungry look in his eyes is a whole other thing. I can't look away.

"Who was at the door?" I ask in a lame attempt to distract myself from the *real* distraction in the room.

"Room service and it looks like crap," he says as the metal lid clanks when he places it back over my salad. "We'll have to order from a better place later. I'm sure you'll have an appetite for something more than salad by then."

"What is going on with you Camden? Why are you doing this? Why are you here?"

Camden stares at me with a look of steely determination.

"Playing stupid doesn't suit you, Jade. You know exactly why I'm here. You've known for weeks. Maybe even months. There's something between us, and we're going to figure out what tonight. No more glares from across the room. No more ignoring me. No more smart-ass comments about who I'm fucking. No more silent treatment at meetings, because you don't know how to communicate when you're pissed."

My head is whirling. "I don't ... I don't want this," I say.

Actually I've wanted this for months, but I've been fighting it. I think it would be a huge mistake that not just the two of us, but all four of us would never recover from.

"Get in the bed," he orders gruffly. "You lie entirely too much."

"Oh my freaking God, you've definitely lost touch with reality—"

"I think you're confused again." He shushes me. "When I tell you to get in the bed, I also mean for you to shut the fuck up."

"Like that will ever happen," I say. Not totally understanding that while my mouth chooses to oppose any and all orders he may give, my body delights in submitting to each and every one of his directives. In other words, I'm fucked.

"No?"

"No," I answer a lot less confidently.

"I've got the perfect way to shut you up. Get on the bed and scoot down. Head away from the headboard."

I follow directions but am shaking while I do.

My heart rapidly pounding.

My breath shortening.

Camden slowly unbuckles the thick leather belt he's wearing with his eyes completely on me. As he pulls the leather through his belt loops, I take a quick inhalation. Frightened that he plans on using the belt on me.

His eyebrow raises in curiosity. "You want the belt, Jade?"

I nod my head no as he chuckles in response. "Next time then."

I stay completely silent as he continues to unzip his pants, and lets them drop to the floor with a thud. My pupils are mono-focused on the growing bulge inside of his black fitted boxers. I think I may have just even licked my lips.

He waits for a moment.

Watching me.

Reading me.

I consider myself pretty tough, and it takes a lot to intimidate a girl like me, but he was doing a pretty good job of it.

When he finally slides his boxers down, I watch in delicious horror as his dick springs completely free. I say horror because I am four eleven, he's got to be at least six two, and his dick is big as shit. I mean I've always suspected it was huge, I've caught glimpses of it in it's flaccid state over the years, but seeing it live, erect, and in person makes what is about to go down between us seem *extra* real.

And fucking scary.

I'm worried.

If the glove doesn't fit, you must acquit, is the only nonsensical line I keep repeating to myself. What if it doesn't fit?

"Wait," is my one-word feeble attempt to stop him, and he does ... after kicking his boxers across the room.

"I don't respond to the word *wait*. The only words you need to say are *stop* if you want this to end or *don't stop* if it feels good. You got me?"

I'm literally speechless as he continues on and climbs carefully onto the bed. Sitting above my head and against the headboard. His dick jutting out and bobbing angrily up and down over the top of my face.

"Hold onto my thighs and open your mouth," he directs.

Fuck, I swear to myself.

I'm so conflicted.

It never dawned on me that Camden would be so commanding in bed. This isn't exactly the way I pictured it in my fantasies. I may have to do whatever he says at work, but in my dreams, I am the one in charge. Taking orders in bed is not something that I'm used to. Not with my one-night stands. With them I always take the lead and I always feel safe. But maybe letting go with someone I am very much attracted to, and someone I trust (to the degree that I can trust anyone) wouldn't be such a big deal. I've done worse things.

So I do what I'm told and grip the outsides of Camden's muscular thighs, while he adjusts himself and then slides his penis into my mouth. Almost immediately I feel another rush of wet heat between my legs. I actually like arrogant Camden King force-feeding his dick into my mouth. *Who knew?* So, surprise surprise, that is yet another one of my rules I'm breaking.

1. No kissing.

2. No fucking the boss.
3. No controlling shit.
4. No fellatio.

Camden begins to gently pump himself in and out of my mouth. Making sure not to move to deeply at first, probably so he doesn't choke me to death. Allowing me to get adjusted to the girth of his cock and the rhythm of his thrusts.

I'm starting to really like this. In fact I want to participate more by at least holding him at the base of his dick or fondling his balls a little, but Camden won't allow it.

"Hands," he reprimands me with a guttural growl when I try to move them. "Back on my legs. *Yes*, Jade, that feels so fucking good."

It's amazing to me how even with my hands basically tethered to his body, holding onto his thighs, that I still feel totally powerful. That I am completely controlling Camden's pleasure with my mouth and henceforth increasing mine as well.

"Spread your legs."

I hesitate at first. I don't want him to see how wet I am. Even though I am enjoying myself, I still can't get completely out of my head. I never do when I have sex. It's a blessing and a curse.

"Wider," he insists.

I take a hard pull on Camden's dick with my mouth as punishment for reprimanding me, but it has the opposite effect. He loves it. He folds his enormous body completely over on all fours and starts licking and lapping me between my legs while pumping himself harder in and out of my mouth.

We are in a perfect sixty-nine position, and for a split second I'm frightened. Probably because I know that I can't control his thrusts in this position. What if he gets excited? What if he starts ramming himself down my throat and I can't stop him? But as these random concerns for my safety swirl around in my head, I can't deny that with each passing moment I feel good. Better than good. My eyes are practically rolling in the back of my head, as we begin to become lost in each other. A sensual and mutual game of tit for tat.

Every time he flicks my clit with his tongue.

I suck him harder.

Every time I take a stronger pull of his cock.

He takes a powerful one of my clit.

It's almost a battle of wills. Who is going to come first? Who is going to scream for mercy first? He's trying to break me, like I'm some sort of wild stallion, not because I believe that he wants me so badly, but probably because there's never been a woman who's told Camden no in his life.

Maybe I serve as some interesting sort of challenge for him, but he's going to realize quickly that there is no way I am ever going to allow him to break me. I will always be free. I will never surrender and become someone's property, someone's plaything, or someone's ATM machine ever again. But if there was anyone ever able to get me to bend my will, God knows that Camden would be the one.

He lightens up on the suction of my clit. Then he bites it.

Then he kisses gently around my core. Almost reverently.

Then rapidly licks back and forth across my clit with his powerful tongue like a human vibrator.

All while holding my legs spread wide and immobile.

It was all beginning to be too much. I was positive stronger women had fallen for less. My legs were beginning to shake, and I swore I could feel my heart pounding through my chest.

"Come for me, Jade," he demands with urgency.

And I come swift and hard like a wild banshee. Screaming expletives and some other unintelligible words, because it feels just that good. Then he comes inside of my mouth with a hushed curse of his own.

"Fuck."

Hot, salty, lava floods my mouth and drips down my throat, but I swallow every drop and am proud that I do. Now I'm hot and sweaty and still very horny. I want more of Camden. So much more. Like him inside of me all over this hotel room, but I refuse to beg for it. Which is what I'm pretty sure he's looking for me to do. He seems the type to get off on begging.

Camden finally lifts his large body from over me and sits against the headboard of the bed staring at me while stroking my hair. It's an odd gesture, because it seems to be part of the post afterglow that lovers share, not two people just fucking around.

The unforgettable orgasm which has totally rocked my body, has me lying here panting for breath, as if I'm unfit and don't run a couple of miles everyday. It must have been the erotic mixture of exertion, adrenaline and bliss making me unusually winded. I can honestly say that no man has ever made me come that hard. I'm already bemoaning the fact that this one-night stand is going to be difficult to put behind me.

"I want to fuck you, Jade, but I'm not going to have my dick inside of you on a Saturday and another man's in there on a Monday."

When he put it that way, he made me sound like a whore, and maybe I was a little, but I liked it that way. Dictating whom I had sex with. Calling the shots about where. Always in charge of the when. Not feeling stifled by relationship restrictions or expectations. And never being disappointed by disappointing men. Yeah, if I had to choose between being a whore and being a pushover then I pick whore all day.

"I'm not sure what you're trying to say."

"It's not a difficult concept. If I'm fucking you, then you're only fucking me."

"Well you're not fucking only me, you're fucking me *tonight*, there's a difference."

He glares at me with icy eyes.

"What are you doing in Baltimore, Jade?"

"Why do you keep asking me that? What do you think I'm doing here?"

"I don't fucking know!" he roars. "That's why I'm asking."

"Huh, you seem upset. I guess all of your little computer programs could track me here, but couldn't tell you *why* I was here. Is that the problem?"

He rubs his face harshly with the palm of his hand in frustration.

"Run the Jacuzzi water again."

"Why?"

"You're going to need it," he says with a maniacal hunger in his eyes I've never seen before.

"I thought you needed assurances that I wouldn't be fucking anyone tomorrow, or the next day, or the next—"

He quiets me with his mouth again.

This time with much more urgency.

And I welcome it.

The warmth of his tongue caressing mine.

A girl could get used to it even though she shouldn't.

"I've decided that I don't want you to make me any empty promises or pledges right now."

He pulls back from the kiss to look directly at me when he speaks.

"Because after tonight you won't want anyone inside of you but me. That I can *assure* you."

JADE

Philadelphia, Pennsylvania
Present Day

I'm doing something that I haven't done in a really long time, and I know I'm probably going to regret it tomorrow, but I'm meeting my younger sister Jana for lunch. I may be three years older than her, but she has always been smarter, more mature, and more successful than I ever have, and she never lets me forget it.

"Has a waiter come over yet?" she asks, while plopping her overpriced handbag on the table.

"Hello to you too, Jana."

"Oh yeah, hi. Happy New Year and all of that. Sorry that I'm a little snappy, but I'm hungry as hell. I had a really long class this morning and skipped breakfast. The professor I work for is so demanding. You're so lucky you didn't pursue this type of career path, Jade."

I have the strongest urge to pluck my sister in the middle of her forehead like I did when we were kids. Jana enjoys throwing in my face any chance she can how she's a teaching

21

assistant for a prominent professor at Temple University, while passively aggressively reminding me of how I barely made it out of high school algebra.

"The server said he'd be right back," I say dryly.

"Is the service here okay?"

She looks around with her nose turned up as if my selection of restaurant is beneath her. As if she has no recollection of how our parents idea of dinner out was a Friday night at McDonald's.

"It's fine," I say with an attitude. "I've eaten here twice before with Roman. You know him right? My *rich* boss."

"Yes, yes, Jade. I'm well aware."

After I flag down our server, a very sluggish boy with freckles and a sandy brown Mohawk (my sister probably isn't too far off about the service here) takes our order.

"Still eating salads every meal I see."

"That's right," I reply smirking. "I need to keep my girlish figure."

This is one of the other things between us. Jana is about twenty-five pounds overweight, and I've always been small and pretty fit, which I attribute to a mixture of good genes, plenty of exercise and a decent diet.

"You could stand to eat a burger or two. You look thin. Too thin. Is that boss of yours working you too hard?"

Jana always tells me stuff like this. I'm used to it by now. That's Jana speak for *you look better than me, bitch.*

"I helped him plan a very romantic proposal to his girlfriend last week, but other than that, work is pretty easy going nowadays."

Our waiter brings us both glasses of ice water with lemon wedges and also a Sprite for Jana. I play around with the lemon inside of my glass as I wait for Jana to get to the real point of this lunch. There's always a point.

"So ... I saw Dad the other day."

I should have seen this coming, but if she was trying to spring a *Daddy* conversation on me, she should have taken me out for drinks not lunch. I need to be totally trashed to talk about that bastard.

"So."

"I think he may be sick. Seriously sick."

I twirl the ice around in my water with the straw, watching as bits of lemon pulp swirl around inside, turning my water cloudy. Like my mood.

"So."

"So ... I think you should go see him."

"And why would I do that?"

"So he can apologize to you before he leaves this earth, which by the looks of him is going to be relatively soon."

I take a long sip of my water. Staring at my sister like the unbelievable turncoat that she is.

"Maybe you were too young to really remember him at his worst, Jana. So I'm going to chalk this conversation up to your youth and ignorance, but let me tell you something ..."

I pull my straw out and point it defiantly at her. She watches as drops of lemon water drip down on the table, driving her absolutely nuts.

"Our father is a motherfucker, and I don't care if he's gasping his last breaths right this very minute. I have no interest in visiting him, talking to him, and certainly no interest in forgiving him."

Her eyes bulge.

"Gosh, Jade, you're so nasty when you're hungry. Where is Mohawk dude with our food? This place is so slow."

"It's worth the wait."

I have a bad habit of sitting on my phone, and cracking the screen at least twice a year. I really need to carry a bag, but I'm a bit of a tomboy and never really got used to them. They just get in my way.

I feel my phone buzzing in the back pocket of my jeans. It's just a feeling, but I think I already know who it is. I thought he had backed off for a while, but now I'm realizing that was just the calm before the storm. He's relentless now.

King Kong: You still avoiding me?
    Me: No
King Kong: You're not?
    Me: I was never avoiding you. I haven't even been thinking about you.
    King Kong: Now we both know that's a lie.
    Me: I'm busy right now. Leave me alone.
    King Kong: Busy doing what?
    Me: Lunch
King Kong: With who?
    Me: My lover. A famous Brazilian soccer player. You don't know him.
    King Kong: That's a very specific fantasy lover :)
    Me: Do you know a real one then? I'd love to meet him.
    King Kong: I'm going to ignore that.

"Are you going to text your fuck buddy during our entire lunch?" Jana interrupts our text exchange like a splash of cold water.

"What are you talking about? Fuck buddy," I mutter.

"I can tell by your facial expressions that you're texting a man. A man whom you have either fucked or want to fuck. You're smiling quite devilishly."

"Lower your voice," I demand.

"Am I wrong?"

"It's just one of the other guys I work for."

"One of those hot twins? Oh my God, are you sleeping with one of them now?"

"They aren't twins," I say flatly. "They're nothing alike."

"Oh, I just assumed. Well which one are you messing around with?"

"We're not messing around."

"Which one were you just angry texting then?"

I sigh.

"The older one."

King Kong: You still there?
Me: What. Do. You. Want.
King Kong: You know what I want.
Me: Is this about Baltimore?
King Kong: It's about me inside of you in Baltimore.

Ugh, he really won't let this shit go, and I'm just about sick of it. I went to the harbor on a fool's errand, but still, it was completely my own business. Then here he comes running after me. Inserting himself in my damn business. Okay so maybe I did slip and fall on his dick in a Baltimore hotel, but while I may not have Jana's book smarts, I have plenty of common sense, and I know better than to do that silly shit twice.

Not going to happen.

No matter how much he pushes the issue.

Me: Stop texting me about this. We have to work together.
King Kong: Or I can work that tight pussy of yours again.

. . .

I'm erasing these messages as soon as I get up from this table. He is so vulgar.

Me: You didn't work it well before, so I pass.

King Kong: Such the little liar. You better bring your sweet little ass to the club by nine, or you and I are going to have a much bigger problem than my dick in your mouth.

Oh my God, I can't stand him. The worst mistake I ever made was spreading my legs for that arrogant, computer hacking, asshole. I mean seriously. He's touched in the head. Completely nuts.

"Where is our damn food?" I slam my phone down on the table livid by the exchange I've just had with Camden and irritated that it takes thirty minutes to get a chicken Caesar salad in this place.

"Excuse me!" Jana turns around and calls out to a group of servers who are by the register. "Somebody better bring us our food real soon or somebody's going to catch a murder charge."

I can't help but laugh. Jana can be pretentious, and a pain in my ass, but sometimes I forget that she and I were raised in the same dysfunctional home. Sometimes some of *that* fire bred into us kicks in. Her approach works too, because lo and behold our food, which evidently had been ready and waiting for Mohawk to pick up arrives.

"Sorry 'bout that," Mohawk apologizes. "We're short staffed today."

"Uh, huh," my sister says unconvinced. "Can you please just bring us some ketchup and some extra napkins? Like right now?" she snaps.

"Of course." He raises one of his eyebrows at that finger snap. "I'll be right back with that."

"He's going to spit in your ketchup." I chuckle. "This is a nice restaurant. It will be easy for him to do it because they bring it in a little dish, not a bottle, and he's pissed with all that finger snapping of yours."

"Nice restaurant my ass."

I take a bite of my salad. It's delicious like I remembered. They make a great Caesar dressing here. No one can pick an out of the way restaurant with great food like Roman.

"So how's school?" I ask, sincerely wanting to know.

"Professor Owens is working my ass off of course. So I've been staying up all night grading tons of papers, and he keeps taking all the credit."

"Well isn't that what teaching assistants do?"

"Yeah, but now that I am one, I see the gross inequality of it all. Seems like everyone in academia works their asses off when they're young, so that one day they can sit back and not have to work at all when they're forty. It's called tenure."

"Isn't that what you want?"

"I guess so. Tenure is part of my fifteen-year plan. Guess I shouldn't deviate from it now."

"Guess not."

"So tell me everything."

"Tell you what?"

"Tell me everything about the twin."

"Not a twin," I say annoyed. I've told her that a million times before.

"Right. What's his name?"

"Camden."

"Right. So tell me about him."

"There's nothing to tell, Jana. You're looking for some interesting love story, but you know that I don't do relationships."

"I know you haven't had any relationships since Tyson, but that doesn't mean you shouldn't. For God's sake, Jade, you two were only kids then."

"I understand that, but it doesn't really matter. I have zero interest in ties or relationships. I work at a place where I meet sexy, amazing men every night. Who wants to be tied down to one man when I'm always in the middle of the best smorgasbord ever?"

Jana puts her fork down for a moment.

"Not every man is horrible, Jade."

I don't look at her and continue eating.

"I never said they were."

"Mom wouldn't want you sleeping with every Tom, Dick and Harry."

This would be the second time I've been called a whore in three months.

"Is that what you think of me, Jana? You think I'm a whore?" I ask defensively.

"Of course not."

"And why bring our mother into this?"

Our mother died when we were just kids from ovarian cancer. She was a warrior. A saint. Bringing her up is just fighting dirty.

"I'm not. I'm sorry I said anything. Just tell me about your boss. I want to know why after he texts you, something lights up inside of you. Like sparklers."

"You watch way too much television. I'm just annoyed. There is nothing *lighting up* inside of me."

"Then why does he *annoy* you so much?"

Jana uses her fingers to form air quote signs while saying the word annoy. Did I mention that my sister is a psychology graduate student? On track to having a rewarding research and teaching career.

"Because he won't leave me alone."

"In a creepy way?"

"No, not like that."

I've called him a creep before, but I'm not going to let my sister think he's one.

"Did you sleep with him?"

Might as well confess. She already thinks I'm a slut.

"Yes."

"Does he want seconds?"

"I don't know what he wants."

"Ah, so that's it. He doesn't just want your body, he wants more."

"He doesn't want more. He's just playing around. He's never been in a serious relationship in his life."

"Ohhh, so he's damaged just like you."

"I don't think he's damaged, and neither am I by the way."

"What's wrong with him then?"

I might as well tell her. She won't stop asking questions.

"I've known him for a long time, Jana. He knows all about Tyson. He was there when it all went down, and Rome got me out of there."

Jana looks down at her plate. This is exactly why I didn't want to talk about this. Anytime I mention Tyson, this guilty look spreads across her face. She and I had a falling out back then. She told me, begged me, many times over to leave my ex, but I wouldn't. At the time I felt trapped. At the time I thought that if I left him, that no one would love me again. My warped thinking and inability to get out of my toxic relationship created a wedge between me and my sister, and we stopped communicating for a long time.

That's why she thinks she failed me, because she wasn't around to help me when the shit really hit the fan. But I don't feel that way at all. She's three years younger than me, our mother was dead, and she was really a kid. It was my job to take care of her and look out for her. Not the other way around.

Unfortunately her guilt, our sibling rivalry, and my inability to put up with a lot of her passive aggressive bullshit is why I have to keep a certain amount of distance from her. I love her, but it's best that we talk occasionally and see each other rarely. Especially since she started speaking to our father again. I want nothing to do with that.

"So are you embarrassed that he knows about that part of your past or something?"

"I'm not embarrassed about anything, Jana. I've accepted that I've made some bad choices. Everyone has. I'm just saying that we know so much about each other. Too much."

"You must be really attracted to him then."

"What? Why do you say that?"

"After everything you just said about what he's seen, and how much he knows, you *still* slept with him. That tells me a lot."

"We all have slip ups now and then."

"I don't believe in accidents, Jade, only fate."

JADE

I stroll into Lotus at 9:23 p.m. on purpose. I know exactly where all the cameras are located in the club, and I know that my creeper is probably watching them from his perch up in the club's office. I stop to talk to Marco, the bar manager. I flirt with him from time to time, because it's just fun. Nothing serious. Nothing that's ever going to lead anywhere.

I can feel *his* eyes on me everywhere though.

Watching me.

Clocking my every move.

He's probably sitting in his chair practically seething, because I'm late. That and the fact that I'm being so cavalier about it. Uh-oh and here comes the other one.

"I think my brother is looking for you, little hobbit," Cutter King says with a mischievous smile.

He calls me hobbit and a million other names as if I don't already know when I wake up everyday that I'm vertically challenged. It just baffles me why all three of these jerks I work for have to remind me of it every single day of my life.

"Why?" As if I didn't know.

"The hell if I know, but it probably has something to do with the fact that he fired Ray today."

Ray is the manager who we never really needed. He kind of did the work that the old manager Larry used to do. Day to day stuff. But with all three of us working out of the club now, and the boys having only a few clients, I don't think there really is a need for Ray. Yet I have an inkling that his firing is about something else entirely.

I make my way upstairs to the club office and knock, something I usually don't do, but I have a feeling that I better keep it purely professional right now.

"Come in," his voice rumbles.

When I enter the office, Camden is sitting at the desk with his laptop open, but the screensaver running. He's not actually doing any work. He's in here stewing about something. When his head pops up and it registers that it's me who's entered the office, some sort of fleeting emotion passes over his face, and then his demeanor returns to normal. Hard. Unreadable.

"You're late."

"You fired Ray?"

"My business."

"Can I ask why you fired him? We didn't need him before, but now that you guys have these new Miami clients, you're going to be stuck doing all the shit work around here and still have to deal with Miami."

"Correction, you're going to have to do the shit work."

"What!?"

"You are now the acting manager of Lotus."

"Oh, hell no, that's not in my job description."

"You don't have a job description. You do whatever the hell we tell you to do."

I suck my teeth.

"That means I'd have to be here almost every day and night of the week, Camden."

"I know what the job entails."

"Roman will never go for that."

"Roman is working the Miami clients, planning a wedding, and having a baby. He doesn't have time to deal with the shit here. Someone needs to handle it."

"So you do it!"

"I have a lot to do for the Miami clients too, and Cutter is handling Mendez on his own. Neither of us has the time to order olives and lemons for the bar or cash out the register."

"Why did you fire Ray then?" I challenge.

"We didn't need him."

I stare him square in the mouth. I locate a spot on his strong, angular jaw that I'd like to punch the hell out of, but I digress. The days of physical altercations with men are over for me.

"Why did you fire Ray, creeper?"

"Why are you calling me names, midget."

"That's politically incorrect, asshole, and not even accurate. I'm short, but not that short, and you are most definitely a creeper. That's just factual."

"I should make you get on your knees right now."

"Shut up."

"You've done it before," he grins.

"I thought we had an agreement. Baltimore never happened. It's been months now, and you need to let it go. Stop texting me about it, stop making references to it, and please stop talking to me like that."

"I never agreed to forgetting shit, and talk to you like what?"

"Like I'm your personal whore!"

Camden stops talking for a moment and quietly studies me in the careful and confident way that he always does. The look that sends shivers down my spine when no one is looking.

"If you must know, I fired him because he was in my way."

"How? In what way?"

He glares at me angrily.

"You *fucked* him, Jade."

"So?"

"So I didn't want to look at his fucking face anymore."

I look down at the floor, but I'm smiling inside. Something about the way he spews his accusation makes me feel warm and jittery. I don't want to feel this way, but I do. He's jealous, and I think that I actually like it. A man lost his livelihood, because Camden was jealous, and I should be outraged. But I'm not.

Regardless of the things said in the heat of passion, I foolishly believed that after he left my hotel room all those months ago, that we had forged some sort of unspoken agreement. That we'd keep our one-night stand between us and not let it affect our working relationship or friendship. But I read Camden completely wrong. He won't let what happened go. And if I don't watch it, I'm going to turn into one of *those* girls who I hate. Girls who ruin themselves over elaborate pipe dreams fueled by meaningless fucks. We can never be more than that one night. That's just common sense.

"I want thirty days," he says to me.

I pop my head up. "What do you mean?"

"Work the manager job for thirty days. If you want to quit after that, you can."

"And what about my work for Roman?"

"Is Roman the only boss you care about?" he asks with an unfamiliar edge to his voice.

"That's not what I meant. You know he's used to a certain level of attention."

"I'll talk to him."

"So all I'll be doing is handling the club?"

"That's right."

"You know this shit is more then just ordering lemons and olives. I don't know if I'll like it."

"That's the point. I don't think you have any idea what you truly want or like." His words are loaded with double meaning.

"I know what you're doing," I say. "But you forget that I know you very well, Camden King. I've watched it happen a million times. I know how this will end."

He closes his laptop and stares at me with a very determined look.

"You have no inkling how this is going to end, itty bitty, because it hasn't really begun yet."

"You know I was drunk that night right? If I had been totally sober I would never have slept with you in Baltimore."

"So that's how you're going to play this?"

"I'm not playing at anything. It's the truth."

"You think I don't know when I'm drunk fucking someone?"

"Oh that's right, I forgot who I was talking to," I say in a snarky voice.

Camden takes me by surprise by practically tossing me on top of the desk and stands in between my spread legs.

"Now that's the first correct thing you've said since you walked in here. You definitely have forgotten who the fuck you are talking to. Maybe I should remind you."

He grabs the back of my neck and pulls me against his warm, hard body. *God, I've missed it.* His strength. His smell.

"You should stop," I say half-heartedly.

"Why, are you *drunk* again?" He smirks.

"This is not going to happen again, Cam."

"Why not?"

His hand slides around my neck and slowly down my chest. He stops at one of my breasts. Rubbing the backs of his knuckles against my nipple. Quickly making it pebble through my shirt.

"You think if you pin me down for a bit of time, that it'll be easy for you to get inside of my head—"

He squeezes my nipple tightly in between two of his thick knuckles. I take a large exhalation in an effort to ignore how good it feels and continue talking.

"Easy for us to fuck like bunnies during this so-called *thirty day* arrangement of yours."

"You said it. I didn't," he says in a deep, raspy voice.

He switches his hand to my other breast, but I keep going.

"You had me once, and now you think you can have me over and over."

"Now you're starting to get it," he replies.

This time he wraps his entire hand around my breast. Massaging it. Gently rubbing the tip of my nipple with his thumb.

"Claim me like a possession," I pant.

"Exactly."

We both hear a door slam across the hall which doesn't particularly startle him, but it does stop him from what he was doing, which then effectively snaps me out of the trance I was falling under. He's convincing, but not that convincing. We made a mistake and had one night of good sex. All right, great sex. But I won't be swayed.

He thinks he knows me. He thinks he can have me anytime he wants. But hasn't he learned his lesson yet? I guess not, but I tell you what, he's about to learn a very long but simple thirty-day lesson.

Jade Barlow is anything but easy.

CAMDEN

The smell of grease and misery hits my senses as soon as I walk inside of Brown's Diner. It's like déjà vu. Roman has already grabbed his "usual" table at his fiancée's favorite hole in the wall, and knowing him he's already ordered me and himself a plate of the grease and salt special.

"Why do you continually force us to meet at this crappy diner?" I ask as I slide myself inside of the cheap pleather booth that probably hasn't been wiped down in weeks. "When did you become so ridiculously sentimental?"

"Watch your mouth. It was your idea to meet today not mine. I'd rather be home inside of my pregnant fiancée. The least you could do is allow us the pleasure of eating at her favorite hole in the wall."

I fake gag.

"Oh would you stop bragging for fuck's sake."

My best friend and business partner has gotten a lot sappier and cockier since he knocked up and proposed to the love of his life. If being cockier is actually even possible for someone as full of himself as he already is.

"You're so obnoxious lately, it's sickening," I add.

Truthfully I'm happy for Rome, but I've got to give him shit about his new life with Elizabeth, because that's how friends like us communicate.

"Once hell freezes over, and you've found a woman who can actually stand you for longer than one night you'll understand."

"Very funny," I grumble. "I take it you already ordered me a turkey burger platter."

"Best thing on the menu."

"I'm pretty sure I've mentioned more than once that I hate those things. Especially the ones from here."

"Nah, I think they're growing on you."

"I assure you that they aren't."

"Do you and Cutter have a handle on the snitch for the case next month?"

"We've got it handled, or at least it will be by the end of the weekend."

"Good."

Roman taps his knuckles on the table to move the conversation along. I guess my pussy whipped friend is not lying when he says he wants to get back to his girl. Plus I think he realizes I'm stalling a bit. I've been avoiding having this discussion for so long, I've allowed the build up to get the better of me. Since when have I ever avoided conflict?

"So what's up?" he asks impatiently. "What couldn't be handled with a phone conversation? Why are we meeting here, eating food you clearly don't want?"

"I fired Ray."

Roman opens his mouth, then snaps it shut, then speaks. "What the fuck do you mean you *fired* Ray? The club is going to need coverage since we're all going to be busy with the Miami job. You promised me that you were on board with this project, Cam, and we don't have time to vet someone new for the club."

"I thought of that. That's why I propose that Jade handle the club. No one knows Lotus better than she does. She can run it with her eyes closed."

Roman smirks. I'm pretty sure the bastard is on to me.

"What's this really about, my friend?"

"Coverage. Just like you said."

"Fucking liar."

Roman squints his eyes a little at me. Analyzing me in an effort to try to unearth what the real story is behind my words. He should know better. Not many people can read me. Cutter perhaps, but not too many others.

"I'm not a mark, Rome. You can't just figure me out with a few scrutinizing glares. We're business partners, and I made a personnel decision about a part of the business that you don't seem to have much time for anyway."

That might have been a little harsh, because I'm trying to deflect, but it doesn't matter. Roman doesn't take the bait.

"Ohhh ... I get it now. Jade *fucked* Ray didn't she?"

I ball up a paper napkin from the table and throw it as hard as I possibly can at his smug face. It's a punk move, but I don't particularly feel like punching my best friend in the mouth in this dump. It's been many years since we were in a fistfight against each other, and I'd like to keep it that way.

"Shut. The. Fuck. Up. Rome."

"What?" He laughs loudly as he swats the napkin away. "Don't get mad at me, because you're permitting Jade to fuck every Tom, Dick, and Harry right under your nose."

"She's a grown woman. She can sleep with whoever she wants."

That shit sounds even stupider flying out of my mouth than it did when I first thought of it, and I guess that's the entire point of this conversation. Even though I *think* she fucked Ray a long time ago, way before what happened between the two of us, I don't want any reminders of the possibility.

"You King boys are real funny when it comes to your women. You and Cutter are super stealth with it. Not as obvious like I am. Guess that's just how you two were raised, and I suppose that's why poor old Ray is jobless now and probably never saw it coming. Marco can't be too far behind either, huh? The way he flirts with the tiny tot all the time; he's bound to get a pink slip too. Although I wouldn't feel too bad about placing that asshole on the unemployment line. I probably should have fired him a long time ago myself. He's got way too much mouth about my woman, and what I do with my woman."

I consider Roman's comments for a moment. It's not like I haven't noticed the way Jade and Marco interact with each other, but so far he's not a real threat. He hasn't made a real move yet, so I've left him alone for the time being. For now I just keep an eye on him and every other motherfucker that breathes her way. I'm very good at watching and waiting for the perfect moment to strike.

"She is *not* fucking Marco."

"Not yet—"

More annoying laughter from the other side of the table as he continues yammering on. He's taking a very sick pleasure in having this conversation. I suppose it was a discussion that was a long time coming. We've danced around it for months. I know he's noticed a thick tension building between me and Jade, especially after we both ended up missing on the day of Juliette's autism fundraiser. He hasn't commented on it though. That's not his style.

"All I'm saying is that I'm sick of you salivating over the little fidget from a distance. It's sickening and totally unnatural. Stake your claim for God's sake. Just don't fuck up what we've got going. The four of us work really well together, and I need us to keep it that way."

Selfish bastard.

"Whatever, asshat."

"I'm saying all of this of course with the caveat that you're actually serious about her."

"I don't play games, Roman. You know that," I declare. "I'm the straightest shooter out of all of us."

"No need to get all sensitive about it, but you ought to cut me a little slack here. You are a straight shooter when it comes to business, but when it comes to women, I can't say that is what I know to be the absolute truth. I've never seen you in any sort of genuine relationship. Ever. You've always had a way with the ladies that was admirable, but never permanent. Jade is not someone that I want you *having a way with* and then breaking her heart. It took us years to put all her pieces back together again."

"I seem to recall that you were the exact same way, if not worse, before you met Elizabeth."

"That's true, but there's a difference. I did what I did in the past, but I made my intentions pretty clear the moment I spotted Elizabeth's pretty ass on the dance floor. You on the other hand have been peeing around Jade for a long ass time. I've never seen someone take so long to mark their territory and claim their woman. There have been sparks flying between the two of you literally since the day you met. I'm wondering if there's a good reason why you waited so long to take the leap."

"She wasn't ready."

"And she's ready now?"

"Circumstances have occurred that have made me force the timeline forward."

"That sounds interesting."

. . .

Our waitress is a thirty-something redhead who introduces herself as Millicent, and even though she's young, she looks like she's seen better days. Sweet though. She's grinning from ear to ear when she delivers our order. Checking us both out like most women her age do.

"Here are your burgers, boys."

"Thank you, Millicent," Roman replies.

I stare at my plate. My burger is some weird gray color, smothered in fried onions and sloppy. Roman is definitely turning into a sentimental jerk, because that's the only thing that could bring him back here like this. The food sucks.

"I think you're overestimating your influence on her," Roman says after taking a bite of his burger.

"What do you mean?"

"Jade doesn't like structure. I don't think she's going to want the job."

"She needs to do what she's told."

He chuckles. "You would think that's how it works, but not with her. You know better than I do that she's a very stubborn woman. As her friend and probably the only man she trusts, I give her a lot of shit, but I also know how far to push her. You may be asking too much."

"She's going to have to learn how to trust more than one man and be more flexible."

"Is that right?" Roman laughs harder. "I'll believe that shit when I see it."

"You'll be believing it soon then."

He chews quietly for a moment then speaks again.

"I have to ask."

"What?"

"What is it about Jade?"

"I don't know. If I did I'd see a doctor about it."

"There's a lot of mouth on that woman."

I take slight offense to that comment.

"And Elizabeth is your cousin. What's your fucking point?"

"There's no need to act like a girl about this."

"You started it."

We both start laughing.

"Since we're in here sharing our feelings like the two little bitches we are, I've got a minor thing to come clean about," Roman says.

"What?"

"I may have mentioned to the glamazon a while back that Cutter is responsible for her not getting any dick lately."

Shit.

"And why would you do that?"

"I needed a bargaining chip."

"So you snitched on my brother?"

He waves me off.

"He's playing around with that girl. He wouldn't have even bothered with doing that shit, if he didn't want her to find out."

"That's your logic for selling out one of your best friends?"

"I'm not talking about this shit anymore. It's done. Thought you should know."

"That's fucked up, Rome."

"Tell me something I don't know. Now pass the ketchup."

"You could do something to make up for your selfishness."

"You fired the manager of *our* club for getting his dick wet, and you call me selfish?"

I'm going to shove this burger down his throat, if he doesn't shut up about Jade fucking that slacker. The imagery is literally making me want to do more than fire his ass.

"Just tell Jade that you want her to focus on the club for now. Don't call her for any of your special little projects, and don't call her for anything Miami related. "

"You know that I call her for all kinds of shit."

"That was before you found Elizabeth. Now you damn near have a wife. You should be asking her to do some of the stuff you ask Jade to do."

"You're asking a lot."

"It's just for a month, maybe two, and you need to stop calling her for all your bullshit grunt work anyway. Jade should have a higher level of responsibility."

"Trusting her with my personal shit is a higher level of responsibility. The highest that there will ever be. I don't trust many people and neither does she. We work well together, because we understand that about each other. She's got her baggage, and I have mine."

"Well you need to start learning how to pack light, motherfucker, and stop thinking only of yourself. I ask you for one favor—"

"All right, *princess*. You're so touchy today." Roman chuckles.

"I'm not touchy, I'm hungry. Do they serve anything in here that's not slathered in onions and grease?"

"I'll make you a deal."

Nothing is ever easy with this dude.

"What?" I ask defensively.

"Come to Miami for a week to handle this Mercer dude with me, and I'll give you your month."

"Mercer."

"He's Kat's biggest client, and he's in the most trouble down there. Bitches, drugs, guns. He's like the Miami police department's wet dream. They're chomping at the bit to nail his ass. So I'm going to need you to work a little of your magic to make some of his problems go away."

"I can do that from here."

"Kat needs to see the magic up close. So she understands how we work. Just one time. Then you can work from Philly."

Normally I don't negotiate with terrorists, but getting Jade to myself, distraction free for a month or two might be worth it.

"So it's an audition?" I ask in disapproval.

"I promised her that she would meet the entire team. She knows me, already met Cutter at the gala, but still has yet to meet you. I wonder why that is?" He smiles alluding to the now infamous Maryland trip that I took in an effort to keep an eye on Jade. Missing my chance to meet Kat in person.

"Give me two months and zero interference from you, and you've got a deal," I say.

"I'll give you one month, minimal interference, with a promise that you're going to tread really fucking carefully, brother. There's a reason why Jade hasn't been in a relationship since that asshole."

"Understood."

"All right then. I'll let Jade know I'm on board with this *plan* of yours, and I'll also let Kat know that you'll be coming to Miami with me. Very soon."

"Yeah, yeah."

"You King brothers will put a motherfucker in the ground when need be, but you're so passive aggressive when it comes to your women." Roman roars with laughter *again* at my expense. I'm so glad I can entertain him.

I admit this is a very unusual position I find myself in, but my gut is telling me that I'm going about this the right way. The way Jade needs me to handle it, so that she doesn't disappear on me completely. She's a fighter, and I need to give her the illusion that she's putting up a good thirty-day fight, so that she can live with the results when she's defeated, and satiated, and happy in my bed.

"Watch your mouth, lover boy, and pass the hot sauce. It's the only way I'm going to be able to get this burger and bullshit you're talking down my throat."

CAMDEN

The King Brothers

S oft swirls of magenta, violet and indigo bathe the city's skyline. It's dusk. My favorite part of the day. The best time for people like me. Night crawlers. After a day of tracking one scumbag named Ronald Patterson, Cutter and I have ended up at the Majestic Hotel & Casino on the Delaware River waterfront where our target has been floundering at the blackjack table for the last forty-five minutes.

The Majestic is a new hotel and casino built as part of the city's expansive revitalization plan for this area of the riverfront. After a huge advertising campaign to attract tourist dollars to the area, the casino has turned around one of the most desolate areas of the city and it continues to rise in popularity among gamblers.

The place is so new that you can smell the faint chemical smell of the green felt rising from the card tables. I myself am partial to casinos that are a bit dated. Casinos that remind you of bell bottom pants, cigarette smoke and lots of gaudy decor. New casinos are sleek and sexy, but they have lots of bills to pay, so you'll never win there. Not big anyway.

I'm not actually surprised that we've ended up here tonight. Ronald has been researching nearby casinos for the past two days on the Internet. My guess is that he's itching to throw away the stack he's been paid to testify against our client. It's amazing what people will stoop to for just a thousand dollars. So I knew it was just a matter of time before he landed somewhere like this. A place that gives him the illusion that he's going to get lucky.

I have to admit, I live for shit like this. The hunting and the gathering. I love what I do for a living, especially when I can do it in one of my custom three-piece suits. Sometimes I get sick of always having to underplay the money I make.

While I know it's important that we live under the radar and not draw attention to our wealth, there are moments I'd like to say to hell with the sweats or jeans and put on a four-thousand-dollar suit, because I can.

Tonight is one of those nights. I'm rocking one of my favorite custom tailored, midnight blue Tom Ford suits with black lapels and a blue and white Windsor knot tie.

I'm probably a little overdressed for this casino, and in particular this table, because there are no high rollers here, but that's all right. I'm going to take a seat, play a few rounds, bankrupt Ronald, then make him an offer he'll have trouble refusing. And by the glances that I'm already getting in this suit, I'll be rounding out the night in a suite drinking a few shots and getting my dick sucked properly, although I'd rather it would be Jade on her knees.

"What the hell is taking you so long?" my brother whispers in my ear. Apparently impatient with my card playing. What Cutter has always failed to realize or had the temperament for is that the first rule of gambling is that you have to wait patiently for your turn of the cards.

I choose to purposely ignore the question or rather his

badgering. I'm counting cards, and it's not something that I do everyday, so for it to work I can't have any distractions.

"I'm talking to you," he whispers again.

I cut my eyes to the side. My signal for him to shut the fuck up, or he's going to pay for it later. I'll never be too old to give my younger brother a good old-fashioned ass whipping.

As I use two fingers to tap the table for another card from the dealer, I notice several women brazenly ogling me, but I only really see one who's worth a second look. A strikingly beautiful woman, with red lips, long legs, jet-black hair, and wearing a modest black jumpsuit at a nearby roulette table.

As she reaches across the table to strategically place her chips down before the ball drops, every man at the table is staring at her ass, and when she places her final chip down, her eyes flick up and catch mine. If this was a couple of months ago, she would have served as motivation to wrap my night up quickly, and get to the better part of the evening.

Funny how things change.

I decide that I've played my last losing hand when I get a text. It's Jade, and for a moment I look away from the game to see what she wants. We haven't talked much since I issued my thirty-day challenge. We've just been keeping things strictly professional, because she hasn't accepted the job at the club yet, and I haven't forced the issue. Time is slowly running out for her though. If I have to be, I can be very persuasive.

Jade: Where are you?
   Me: Busy.
   Jade: Are you coming to the club?
   Me: Probably not. Why? You want to see me?

· · ·

Cutter whispers in my ear again.

"Pay attention."

I cut my eyes towards him a second time, but again I don't say anything to my brother. I never like to react to someone speaking to me in the middle of a hand. Not only is it a distraction, but it allows other players an insider look into my mood. A definite no-no when you're playing cards, even though this is basically an amateur table.

I text Jade again since she hasn't responded to my last message, and because I'm wondering if these texts are her ass backwards way of agreeing to my proposal.

Me: Do you *need* something?
Jade: No, never mind, I'm good.

I'm no idiot. I know Jade. I've been inside of Jade. She doesn't text for no reason, but if she doesn't want to tell you something, then she won't. She's stubborn like that. So I decide to get back to what I'm supposed to be doing, before Cutter fucks it all up with his impatient interruptions.

I can sense that Ronald is starting to feel pretty confident about the rising stack of chips in front of him. His last few winning hands have lulled him into a false sense of security, because now he's trying to beat the house using a betting progression strategy. A fatal blackjack mistake.

Based on the time we've sat here, the number of players at the table, and the number of cards that I've counted, there's a high probability that Ronald's hand is good, but that I'll have the winning hand.

So I bet high.

I bet everything I've got on the table.

That's Cutter's cue to walk away and head to the bar,

because that's where our devastated loser will probably be headed after he's lost this hand. I've done the intel, and he has a thing for taking shots of expensive vodka after he's finished playing cards.

The dealer flips over Ronald's final card. He's a bust with a total of twenty-four.

Then she turns over my final card.

"Twenty-one wins."

Okay, so sometimes these scenarios play out exactly like I plan, and sometimes we have to go off script. I won the hand and several thousand dollars, and Ronald lost his entire pot, but the jackass didn't head straight to the bar like my intel suggested he would. He made a call instead that sent him straight out of the casino and over to the valet to call for a cab.

"What now, Sherlock?" Cutter asks sarcastically.

"Obviously we need to grab him before he gets in a car."

"Obviously. So who's going to do it? You or me?"

"Me. You get the car and bring it around here. And get my boots out of the trunk. I need to get out of these shoes. Dress up time is over."

I approach the valet stand and ask them to fetch a fictitious Jaguar. When one of the guys returns to say that he can't find it, I act as if I am going to cause a serious scene which gains the attention of the manager.

"I'll search for it myself, sir. My apologies for the wait."

I nod in acknowledgement of his efforts, especially because this leaves the desk unmanned for a while. Best time to confront Ronald. Just in case I have to hurt him to get him into the car, I don't want any do-gooders calling the cops.

"Finished for the night?" I ask casually.

He glares at me for a moment. Remembering that I'm the guy who wiped him out at the blackjack table.

"You won a lot of my money, so yeah, I'm finished."

"I know a way you can get it back."

The look on his face questions my motives, but as I was counting on, he's too desperate to walk away.

"I'm listening …"

~

Turns out Ronald wasn't that interested in listening at all, in fact he got a little indignant after I made my offer, as if I offended him. So now I'm spending the rest of my night in the middle of a freezing, abandoned, concrete building that smells like motor oil, piss, and mold.

Crushing this asshole's head under my boot.

My glock pressed against his temple.

My brother is trying to reason with him, while I hold him helpless on the ground. His words are a sheer waste of time in my opinion. I've always told Cutter that there's no point in reasoning with someone who lacks basic intelligence and this guy is dumber than dirt.

All the dumbass had to do was take the three grand I offered him to walk away from testifying, also widely recognized as snitching, at an upcoming case for one of our clients. A very simple transaction. An easy yes. But simpletons like to make things difficult sometimes, and this guy was no different.

Instead of taking the money and walking away, he actually tried to stab me with a pocketknife that was stashed inside of his jacket. As if that would have ever worked. I've had fourteen-year-old punks come at me that were smarter and faster than this dummy.

"This is real stupid, homeboy." My brother bends over to say to the pissant. "You should've just taken the money, and you definitely shouldn't have tried to shank him. Now look at what you've done."

I guess I should give Ronald a little credit. He doesn't budge. He doesn't plea for his life. He doesn't once speak up to say that he's changed his mind about testifying. He just quietly grimaces while I dig the heel of my boot into the side of his face. Actually his tough guy act is pissing me off. I had no intentions of beating his ass and getting blood on my favorite suit tonight, but now he's making me think otherwise.

A text buzzes my phone to life. It's Jade again. Two messages on the same night from Jade is not standard fare. I stare at her text a little longer than I normally would. Trying to assess the hidden meaning behind her innocuous message this time and the inquisitive one from earlier. In fact, my eyes are actually glazing over my phone screen, in an attempt to decipher the subtext of her brief message, *call me when you're done,* when I hear the two deadly clicks near the back of my head.

Shit.

Two clicks means that there are at least two motherfuckers who followed me and Cutter into the warehouse, and they are holding at least two guns on us right now.

CAMDEN

"Get your foot off the boy, put your gun down, and walk away slowly," ordered one of the men. Clearly someone older if he considers the douche on the floor the age of a *boy* rather than a grown man.

Cutter is bent down in front of me, but turns his head slightly towards the voice, and when he does I recognize the fury in his eyes. He's just as pissed as I am that there are two guns on us, but more importantly that we've fucked up like this.

We're fixers and we know better. It's our job to clean up messes made by the wealthy clients who hire us. It's a vocation we were born and bred for. We're good at it. And even though it can sometimes get complicated, and messy, and dangerous, we don't usually make mistakes like this. But tonight we did.

"Who the fuck are you?" Cutter demands to know while backing away carefully his hands up in the air.

I on the other hand still have my gun pointed at Ronald. It's going to take more than a simple request from some old dickhead for me to relinquish my piece. Especially when there's a gun pointed at my own damn head.

"Never mind who I am, and I'm not going to say it again. Get your foot off of Ronald's head, put your gun down, and back away, or I'll blow a hole through the back of both of your skulls."

Without even having to look at me, Cutter knows that I am not going to back down. We've been raised if someone puts a gun to your head, then you better put his ass in the ground.

Whoever this is has balls, is smart, and must have been following us for a while to have cornered us in this out of the way location without us knowing. Which also means that we have no clue what he knows and what he doesn't. Another complication and a loose end.

While we rarely have to resort to lethal force in our line of work, one thing that this job doesn't tolerate is loose ends. Especially loose ends that put a gun to your head. Unfortunately you can only tie up loose ends with money or with blood.

Ronald already turned down our money.

So tonight it would be blood.

I keep my foot on Ronald's head, but bend down slowly to place my piece on the floor. Giving the gunman the illusion that I am fully cooperating. I place my hands up and after giving Ronald's head one more hard squish with the bottom of my boot, I slowly begin to back away.

I make sure to back myself up completely in front of Cutter, so that I am standing directly in front of him. Like we're in a line. Both of us with our hands up. Then we both turn to face the gunmen to get a good look at their faces. They don't look familiar, and they don't look like professionals, but they do look very motivated. This Ronald guy means something to them. Maybe he's family.

"Get up, Ronnie," the other man orders. Answering at least one question of mine. This *is* personal. They definitely know him. They have a nickname for him. *Ronnie.* Which means that my brother and I are probably as good as dead if we don't handle this situation carefully and swiftly.

"Now go outside and get in the silver Lincoln. We'll be out in a minute. We just gotta take care of these two shitheads."

Ronnie stands up, brushes off his pants, and nods his head smugly. I can feel it in my gut that this is going to go down quickly. The minute Ronald makes it to the other side of the door we're going to be put six feet under by these two middle-aged Rambos. They're not professionals, but I can tell they've killed before. It's much easier the next time.

It's obvious we're going to have to shoot our way out of this one. I just pray that Cutter remembers how we made it out of a situation like this once before, and the reason why I'm standing so closely in front of him.

Fortunately for us he does.

And it all goes down in a matter of seconds.

As Ronald opens the door to leave, Cutter quickly steps closer behind me, reaches inside of my jacket and under my shirt, where I carry a second gun. I always carry two when I'm working.

He whips the small Beretta Pico out of the back of my waistband, carefully takes aim over my shoulder and in between my raised arms, then shoots both men in the head with two quick shots using marksman precision.

Pop! Pop!

While we take the man in charge completely by surprise, the other gunman sees it coming and tries shooting first. Not quickly enough though. Fortunately the asshole's safety jams, and they both collapse to the ground before he can get a shot off. Cutter rarely misses his mark.

As soon as their lifeless bodies hit the ground, Ronald shrieks like a little girl. "Barry! Oh my God, No!" he screams while running to the guy that gave the orders just moments before.

I pick my glock back up and breathe for a moment. We're alive, and for that I'm grateful, but I'm also pissed. This very simple bribery job has morphed into a big pain in my ass. Now we have a clean up situation. I hate those, because you basically have to make a scene look like you were never there. No bodies. No DNA. No evidence whatsoever. And that shit is much harder to accomplish than you would think.

To execute a drama free clean up and cover up you either have to have a friend in the police or coroner's office, know an actual criminal *cleaner* for hire, or do the job yourself. None of us have connections to the coroner, and a professional cleaner is hard to come by at the last minute, so we decide to handle the shit ourselves.

Arson would be the easiest way to go in this situation. The warehouse is abandoned and there are no other buildings open within a two or three block radius at this time of day. So there won't be any innocent bystanders getting hurt by a fire, or anyone to call and stop the blaze before it effectively wipes away any traces of our DNA.

I turn the gun back on Ronald while Cutter makes a call to Roman, to give him a heads up about what's going on. This type of thing is usually up his alley, but he's been preoccupied lately.

"You see what you've done, *Ronald*," I say coldly.

Tears start rolling down his face.

"He was my brother!" he wails. Snot running down his nose.

"Boo fucking hoo. You'll see him soon in hell or wherever snitches go if you don't do what we asked you to do. What we offered good money for you to do thirty minutes ago.

This is all on you, you know that right? You've turned this into way more than it needed to be."

"You're a fucking maniac!" he yells at me with his eyes wide in disbelief and disgust. "You both are!"

"Because we shot first? How convenient of you to dismiss the fact that your beloved brother was about to put both me and *my* brother in the ground. He was no fucking saint."

"He's never killed anyone in his life. He wouldn't have—"

"Really, man? On top of everything else, you're also naïve? Your brother had a gun cocked and pointed at my head, and so did his friend. In my world that means he was ready to take a shot. He made his choice, and it was a bad one. Now it's done. He's gone. And you still have a job to do, or you'll be gone too. Take the money and go far away, *or* I'll just make you go far away."

"Can I speak to you for a minute?" Cutter interrupts after finishing up the call with Roman. I already know what he wants. At this point there's no way I should still be giving Ronald the option to take the money, and my brother wants to check me on it.

We've ended two lives tonight. Two people connected to a guy that knows us. Knows what we look like. Knows what we do for a living. Knows the client we work for. He could easily incriminate us. The reality is that we have to eliminate Ronald too. I just don't want any more blood on my hands. Not tonight.

Ronald looks back and forth between us with terror in his eyes, especially when he looks at my brother. Cutter was the one who actually took the shots tonight, so in Ronald's eyes Cutter is the bad cop, and I am the good cop, or at least sort of good.

"Wait!" he turns to me and begs for his life. "I'll take the money. I'll go far away. Out to the west coast. Wherever. Just don't kill me."

"Have a seat against the wall over there. Let me speak to my brother about it," I say.

I can see the hope in Ronald's eyes.

It is very much misplaced.

I'm no good cop.

There'll be no discussion.

It was already decided the minute he tried to shove a knife in my gut.

~

I'm in my office at the club, and I smell like accelerant and smoke and sweat. I'm fucking exhausted. I've committed about a dozen crimes tonight, and while that wasn't something that used to bother me, I'm starting to think that as I grow older, I'm getting softer. Or maybe it's simply a case of me preferring to do what I do best.

Tracking and hacking.

Learning who people are, what they do, what they buy, and where they go by digging into personal emails, phone records, and work databases. Gathering intel that we can hold over them and get what we want without having to resort to blood. It's so much easier, and it doesn't sit on my chest like a crushing weight for days, like the shit we did tonight will.

I start backtracking the way we handled this job from start to finish. Our old boss, Joseph Masterson (Roman's father), taught us very early on that everyone has a price, and our job is always to find it. Maybe three grand wasn't Ronald's price. Maybe if I hadn't let the knife he tried to put in my side piss me off so much, and interrogated him a little further, I would have discovered his *real* price.

I guess I could second-guess myself all night, but what's done is done. There will be no testimony made by him incriminating our client, and therefore we have fulfilled our end of the contract. *How* we fulfill it is on us. Not the client. That's our burden to bear.

"You look like hell," Jade notices, but I don't respond to my little foul-mouthed distraction. I'm too fucking angry with myself for all the mistakes we made to spar with her tonight. Especially the one which almost allowed two amateurs to get the drop on me and Cutter.

"And I told you to call me when you were done," she continues fussing.

I start to mindlessly rummage through my duffle bag for some sweats to change into. I don't even look at her when I respond. All I want to hear her say is that she'll agree to my terms. She's pissing me off by taking so long.

"You don't *tell* me to do anything. You'd do best to remember that shit."

"What the hell crawled up your ass, King Kong?"

I pop my head up and look at her straight on.

"Didn't I tell you to stop calling me that shitty nickname?"

"As if I like any of the names you call me."

"What you like or don't like is not important." I'm being an asshole, but there's something about our acerbic exchanges that always lifts my mood.

"And what are you wearing?" I ask as I run my eyes up and down her body. Questioning why she's wearing skintight leggings and a cut off shirt, which puts all of her delicate curves on full display for every man to ogle. "Leggings are not pants."

"What are you my daddy? When I'm not at Roman or Elizabeth's house, I work inside of an office at a nightclub, genius. You're lucky I don't wear a g-string all day."

I should be so lucky.

"I can see the imprint of your crotch."

"Why are you even looking down there? Keep your eyes above my neck. That should help."

"You're distracting the men that work here dressed like that."

Jade laughs. "They see half naked women every night, and you're worried about them looking at me? Look at me," she demands incredulously.

That's the problem. I *am* looking. I'm always looking.

"I'm totally covered up, and I don't even know why we're having this conversation," she blusters. "I can wear what I want. Even if I was walking around here in the nude, these guys should still do their jobs."

"Now *you* sound ridiculous."

"Male employees do it at strip clubs everyday."

"They're all gay."

"No they aren't." She laughs out loud.

"Well this isn't a strip club."

"And there's never been a dress code here except for wearing all black. Since when do you care what I wear to work anyway?"

"You ever heard of dressing for the job you want and not the job you have?"

I'm bullshitting so much right now, that I can smell my own self. I haven't felt this territorial about a woman since ... never. It's embarrassing.

"So what? You want me to look like all of the corporate bitches that come sniffing around here for you every night? In silk sheath dresses. Pant suits. Ugly ass kitten heels. Is that what you want?"

She's right about one thing. I do tend to attract the corporate types. Beautiful college educated women who come to Lotus for the overpriced mixed drinks and fantasies about getting their bad boy fixes met by fucking one of the notorious owners. But Jade's clueless. That's not what I want by a long shot. I don't want corporate. I want her.

"No, Jade. Just cover up your ass."

"Why don't you just forget about my ass. How about that."

I wish I could.

"I texted you earlier for a reason," she says getting back to the original topic.

"What was it? I was too busy making sure I didn't get myself shot in the head."

"What else is new. Look, I'm taking the day off tomorrow."

"That's what you wanted? The day off," I respond in disbelief.

"Yes, yes. I know it's unheard of at this company," she says in a condescending tone. "But at most places, employees actually get vacation days that they can use for whatever the hell they want."

"You don't."

"Well, I am tomorrow. I've already cleared it with Roman, so I'm letting you and Cutter know too. You'll have to manage without me tomorrow."

I try not to ask, but the words tumble out of my mouth.

"What are you going to do tomorrow?"

I'm such a bitch.

"You're so nosy. No one asked me a single thing about what I'm doing but you."

"Just wondering what would make you take a day off of work. What couldn't wait?"

"Wait until when? The weekend? You've got to be kidding me. Between the clients and the club, I work seven days a week. It's got to be illegal how many hours I log weekly for you guys."

"Fine, take your stinking day off," I say, frustrated with the direction of the conversation.

She snickers, "I wasn't asking for your permission or approval. I was just letting you know."

"You do remember that you work for *me* right?" I grumble while ransacking my duffle.

"You never let me forget it."

"When are you coming to work here full time?"

"I'm not."

"Ungrateful brat." *Dammit, I don't have any clean underwear.* "I'm running home for an hour. Can you at least do your job while I'm gone."

She laughs, "Go take a shower while you're there. You stink like badly burnt barbecue."

When I get up to leave, I can't help myself.

Her tits are covered up, but IT is staring at me.

Taunting me.

Jade's ass.

I give it a good slap as I make my exit, and oh my fucking hell, I forgot that it jiggles.

"Hey!" She jumps in protest.

"See you later, itty bitty." I grin. "And if you don't want anyone to touch it, maybe you should cover it up."

I laugh as I listen to her spew a string of curse words behind me. Something about perversion and workplace harassment, but the joke was really on me. My hand, her ass, and my dick all just shared a mutually beneficial connection that reminded me of why I want her here with me twenty-four seven. I can't get the picture of that *jiggle* and the way it felt against my hand out of my head.

I'm burdened with the desire of wanting more.

I just hope she'll put me out of my misery soon.

JADE

I've been staring at the blank screen of my cell phone for ten minutes. Trying to decide whether or not I'm going to call Roman, the police, or no one at all. There's a dark blue Honda sedan parked directly across the street from my apartment building. Facing my living room window. The car has tinted windows, the lights are off, and it's been in the same exact space all day for three whole days.

Sometimes I see the silhouette of a man sitting inside. Sometimes the car is empty. I never really get a good look at the guy getting in or out, but if I had to guess, the jackass is purposely trying to spook me.

My bosses are partners in a company that provides a very specialized service for rich bastards who can afford to pay them to clean up messy situations. I help them do that in whatever way they need me to. They usually try to tie up loose ends when we do a "fix" for a client, but there have been a few things that may have fallen through the cracks here and there, and the owner of this blue Honda parked across from my place may just be one of those things that has fallen through the cracks.

A disgruntled customer perhaps?

Yet somehow I think if there was an axe to grind or revenge to be had against us, someone would be smart enough to go after the weakest link in our circle—Roman's cousin Elizabeth. You fuck with her and all hell will break loose. Fuck with me? Not so much.

If I was actually following protocol, I should have already told one of the guys about the Honda, but I'm not actually *that* worried about the car—I'm just curious. That's why I took the day off. I'm going to do a little of my own detective work today, and find out who the hell is in this car, so I can get some actual sleep.

What does this guy want?

Is he planning to break in?

Beat me up?

Am I even on his radar, or am I being paranoid?

Maybe this isn't connected to my job at all. Maybe he's watching another apartment. Maybe he isn't watching anyone at all. Hell, for all I know he could be living in that Honda. I could be starting trouble for a homeless man. It's very possible that I'm being over suspicious, because I've been working for those three crazies entirely too long.

I took the day off to figure this thing out myself. No need to bother anyone else. Especially Roman. He's got a million things on his plate right now since the engagement and baby news, and there's no need to involve the police, because they wouldn't do much of anything until the guy actually tries to kill me, or something.

Maybe a little exercise will get my mind off of things. It's four o'clock anyway. Close to the time for me to meet my trainer at the gym. After Ryan puts me through an excruciating hour of lunges, squats and a few other bootcamp-like drills, I run for twenty minutes on the treadmill, and then head home after I get a call from Roman.

"Hey, what's up?" I answer the phone a little too enthusiastically. Hoping he has something for me to do. This day off was a waste of time.

"You bored already?"

"Nope."

"Liar."

"Do you actually need something?"

"Well I ain't calling to swap green drink recipes or talk shit about men."

"That's not all I talk about, jackass."

"I need you to make a run."

Thank God. A reason to stop driving myself crazy with this Honda business.

"Where?"

"I need you to grab a couple of things for me at the mall. I'll text you a list and the stores that they're at."

"The mall?!"

I hate the mall, and so does Roman. The only thing he could possibly want there would be shit for his fiancée. I pop the wad of gum in my mouth loudly a few extra times, because I know it gets on his nerves, and because this isn't the type of "run" I was hoping for.

"You actually think I'm your personal assistant don't you?"

"Yes the hell I do, because you are."

"I'm not *her* assistant."

"You're right, you're mine, and if I ask you to go to the mall, then you go to the mall."

"I don't do grunt work."

"We've been over this ad nauseam. I'd be totally interested in hearing what exactly you think your job title and description are if it ain't to *do whatever the fuck I tell you to do*."

This type of banter has always been part of my relationship with Roman and the King brothers. We're friends first, close friends, but they're also my employers. So I try my best never to cross a line with them, but it's difficult sometimes. The lines can get blurry. Especially because they all have such strong personalities, and I'm a woman who's never going to act like some meek little assistant without a brain or an opinion. That's just not who I am.

"Slave would be a more accurate title," I deadpan.

"Slave's don't get wages."

"You're always throwing your money in my face, rich boy."

"Yet you seem to cash the checks every single damn week."

"Whatever. Just text me what I need to get. It better not be thongs or something gross for your *cousin*. Oops I mean … fiancée."

"You're cruising for a bruising."

"Cruising for a bruising? Gah!" I laugh out loud. "My nana use to say that, old man, and that was a hundred years ago."

"One more thing, Jade."

"What else?"

"This is going to be your last personal run for me for awhile. We need you to take the reins over at Lotus until we get a handle on this Miami job."

"What?"

I can't believe it. That freaking Camden.

"Just for a month or two. Three months tops."

"How convenient."

"What are you talking about?"

He's playing stupid.

"Will today count as day one?" I ask calling his bluff.

"If Cam says it does, then it does."

I knew it.

"So *he's* in charge now?"

"The Kings and I run a partnership. This isn't like Masterson & Associates where we all worked for Joseph, and I was the heir apparent. It's different now. We make decisions equally. If he says we need you at the club, then we need you at the club. If Cutter said that he needed your help with Mendez, then you'd probably be helping him with Mendez. Is there a problem?"

Why is he playing this game with me? I know he's suspected for the longest time that something happened between me and Camden. Hell, Cam may have even told him. I don't know what those blockheads talk about when they're out on Roman's boat fishing and drinking.

"Roman," I whine. "I don't want to be stuck inside of that club all day everyday. I'm there enough as it is. I'm going to kill somebody, if I don't feel the sun on my skin on a daily basis."

"Kill somebody in particular I bet." He chuckles.

How can the two of them be so shamelessly in cahoots with each other?

"First you send me on an errand for your *cousin*, and now you want to stick me in a dark office all day with the King brothers. What have I ever done to you to deserve this treatment?"

"I think what you meant to say is that I'm sending you on an errand for my *fiancée* and the future *mother* of my child, *and* that I'm giving you the honor and privilege of running the hottest club in the city."

I pull the phone back from my face, look at it, and roll my eyes.

"See how I reframed that?" he asks loud enough for me to still hear.

"Bastard."

"Hanging up now, munchkin," he says with an irritatingly chipper voice. "Will send you that text shortly."

Watching Roman fall in love has probably been one of the funniest and most ridiculous things I've ever witnessed, and it's changed him. I mean who in their right mind falls in love with their cousin? Okay—step cousin or cousin by marriage but whatever. She's more family to him than I am, and I would never sleep with him. I mean he's hot and all, but *ewww*, that's just a line I would never cross. Of course that's the same thing I would have sworn about Camden a few months ago, and now look at me. Stuck working with him for thirty days, so that he can attempt to get inside of my panties again. As if I'd ever be that stupid a second time.

After I shower to rid myself of the bad juju that's clearly following me around, I get a call from Camden which makes me seriously consider the magnitude of what I'm going to be dealing with over the next thirty days of my life.

A man that's always in my business.

Always watching me.

Terribly judgmental.

Extremely overprotective.

And I suppose that I should add that he's also ridiculously sexy.

Even before sleeping with him, there was no denying it. Out of my three employers, Camden King has been the most blessed with all of God's good intentions: body, brains, and badass swagger.

"Hey, itty bitty."

"What's up, King Kong?"

"Heard you're taking a mall run."

"Did your boyfriend tell you that, or are you tapping my phone calls now?"

Camden is a technical genius with an extremely curious nature. I wouldn't put it past him and his stalkerish tendencies to have tapped all of our cell phones (for our own good of course); although I wish he'd use his superpowers for good, like breaking into the TransUnion or Equifax's servers and fixing my shitty credit report.

"Funny."

I place Camden on speakerphone, so I can multitask. I'm slathering on some lemon body butter and continuing to keep an eye on the Honda from my window. It's still light outside this time of year, so I'm hoping to catch a sighting of Mr. Mysterious before I head out.

I audibly gasp when I notice a hooded man, with an average build, walk across the street towards the car and then turn around and look directly towards my window before getting inside.

"Shit."

Our eyes momentarily meet, and I try ducking down to shield myself from his view.

"What is it," Camden demands to know sternly on the other end of the phone. "What's wrong?"

Dammit, I didn't mean to say that out loud.

"Nothing."

"What do you mean nothing?"

"Calm down. It's fine."

"Don't lie to me."

"I swear. I was just getting dressed in front of an open window, and I think some weirdo saw me. It's my fault. I should have had the shades down."

There's a moment of dead silence making me think momentarily that the call dropped.

"You don't have any clothes on?"

"Uh, no, true detective," I wisecrack. "I just got home from the gym. Had to take a shower before I go on this senseless, pointless mall run. Rome texted me the list of stuff

I need to buy. It's all for his new princess. Nothing to do with the club or a client."

"Get on board, Jade, and stop giving him so much shit about it. She's part of the package now. He's in love. Love can be a good thing."

"Oh, stop it. Love? He's not in love. He's just bored from banging socialites and actresses."

"Such a cynic."

"I don't think you're in a position to speak on this topic. Since when have you ever been in love?"

"I'm in love every other night."

"You're so gross. I feel so buried beneath all of your crap right now, that I forgot the original nature of your call."

"That mouth of yours. Does it ever shut up?"

"Never."

"That's what I thought. Listen, the *original nature* of my call as you so put it was to let you know that this is your day one as manager of the club, and I'll be at your place in the next ten minutes."

"I didn't agree to become manager."

"That's not the way I heard it."

"You guys suck."

"Like I said, I'll be at your place in the next ten minutes."

"What in the ham sandwich for?"

"To take you to the mall and then from there we can head over to the Lotus. Your car is a piece of shit, and I know you're not trying to Uber all the way to the mall. That'll cost a fortune."

"A cost that my employers will pay for, so what do I care?"

"I have a parts run to make over that way anyway. I'll just come by and scoop you."

I don't want Camden to come to my house for a lot of reasons, but mostly because he'll probably notice a strange guy sitting in a parked car in front of my window, and he won't sit around and watch him like I've been doing. He'll probably just go crack the windshield with a baseball bat or the butt of his gun and tell him to fuck off.

That's one of the things that can be so deceiving about Camden. He can often be expressionless, quiet, pensive, but he's also ripped, smart and dangerous as fuck. He can sit silently for hours on his computer and dig for information, but in the real world he has very little patience for people. He only wants to ask a question once. He only wants to explain something once. He only wants to deal with a problem once. And he doesn't like mistakes.

"I'll meet you near the mini-mart. The one on fifth," I say hoping he'll buy my bullshit.

"I can just pick you up at your house, Jade."

"No, no. I'm on my way out the door as we speak. I'll see you there in fifteen."

"A minute ago you were naked by the window." He sounds perturbed.

"I get dressed quickly. Mini-mart. Fifteen minutes."

"You sure everything's all right? If you lie to me—"

"Everything's fine."

"You're so damn weird. Fine, I'll see you in fifteen."

I'm bent over outside of the front door of my apartment building, popping two pieces of spearmint gum, and lacing up my Converse while I get a really good look at the blue Honda. This close up I can see that Mr. Mysterious is in there. He's in the driver's seat, which is tilted far back, and there's some sort of hand towel covering his entire face. As if he's trying to keep the sunlight out of his eyes for a nap.

It's going to drive me completely crazy if I don't finally confront this guy. Hell, I actually took a day off of work to do it. Maybe he needs my help? So I start walking towards him. He must have been watching me the whole time or has some crazy peripheral vision, because he snatches the towel from his face and rolls down the window as I approach.

His face is blank.

Eyes kind of dead.

I can't read him at all, mostly because he doesn't want me to.

I quickly scan his face, as well as the interior of the car, for any signs of drug use or paraphernalia, but I don't see anything. His skin looks clear. His eyes aren't red. No pipes, blunts, rolling papers, or pills. He's definitely not homeless, but there's something about him that looks faintly familiar and not in a good way. I just can't put my finger on what it is.

"What the fuck do you want?" Is the first thing I ask him. Hands on my hips. Attitude rolling off of me.

Silence

"What's your name?" I try again.

Still nothing.

"Are you stalking me or something? Do you know who you're fucking with?"

The stranger finally responds to my brief interrogation with a smirk.

"I know *exactly* who I'm fucking with," he replies. "And it's a pleasure to finally meet you, Miss Barlow."

That voice. I've heard it before.

"Do I know you?" I ask looking around. Worried that I may have fallen into some sort of trap.

"No, but we have someone in common."

"Who could we possibly have in common?"

"Someone who's lived a lifetime of regrets."

That could be a zillion people. I don't have time for a fishing expedition.

"Not interested."

"Are you sure?"

"I'm so sure, dude."

I turn to walk towards the direction of the mini-mart when the stranger calls out.

"Even if it's my brother, Tyson?"

Five Years Ago

W*HACK!*
He hit me.
Hard.

I quickly placed my palm across the left side of my face. My skin felt tingly, was hot to the touch, and I swear to God for a few moments I really thought that I could hear bells ringing in my ear. It hurt like hell, but before I took too much time to wallow in the intensity of the searing pain, I lifted my head back up, remembered the girl my mother raised me to be, and promptly kicked my boyfriend Tyson in his nuts.

I'm pretty sure I heard him yelp the words "you bitch" on his way down, but the point was he was on his way down to the ground. Right where he belonged. I was in no fucking mood to fight with him that day.

I had just gotten a call from my little seventeen-year-old sister asking me for a referral to a gynecologist. She wanted birth control. I didn't even know she had a boyfriend. I felt like dog crap. I was doing a horrible job of being a role model for Jana. My mother was probably rolling over in her grave.

"Are we done?" I asked a moaning Tyson.

He was such a whiner. I didn't even kick him that hard. Then I realized that he must have been high. And when he got high on junk like ecstasy, his dick always got hard, which made the kicking of his balls even more painful. Great for me, but not so nice for him.

"Not by a long shot, bitch."

I really got annoyed then, because I knew him calling me a bitch meant that he was ready for a knock down, drag out, reality show like sparring match. Which would mean that part of my face was going to end up a nasty shade of purple by the end of the night, and I'd have to dig into my makeup kit once again. A kit filled with theatrical face cover. Cover that I paid a lot of money for, but couldn't really afford, so I only wanted to use it if I absolutely had to. I know. That line of thinking was totally fucked up, but I was young and dumb and had no one telling me any better.

Tyson hit me that night, because I dared to ask him if he took the forty-five dollars that was in a sealed white envelope inside of my underwear drawer. At the time I was working as a waitress, and had been saving the money to buy a gift for Jana's eighteenth birthday. It was a lot of money to both of us back then, and his response to my question told me everything. He had stolen the money, and it wasn't too difficult to see why. He had bought drugs with it. Something his miserable ass had been doing more often than not, but I had been too stupid to jump ship before it got completely out of hand.

~

I met Tyson when I was just fifteen years old. I had been outside with some friends from the neighborhood for practically the entire morning. It was hot that day. Humid, swamp like heat. So we took a ten-minute bus ride to the local mall and wandered in and out of stores all day to keep cool.

He was working as a stock boy in the Hallmark card store when he stopped me dead in my tracks while I was looking at the Christmas in July display. I was examining figurines. I loved those things. They reminded me of my mother and my nana. Two women who lived for Christmas, two women whom I loved, and two women who were long gone from this earth by then.

"You going to buy that?" he asked me.

I knew he wasn't old enough to be the manager or even assistant manager of the store, so I gave him a little attitude, because basically I thought he was an ass for assuming that I was a thief or that I was too broke to buy one crappy figurine.

"What business is it of yours?"

"I spent all morning putting those on the shelves in a very specific order."

I looked at the display.

Then at him.

"They don't look like they're in any sort of order to me."

"Well they are."

"Come on, Jade, he's so rude." My girlfriends cackled as they pulled me out of the store.

"But so hot," one of them said loud enough for him to hear.

"See you later, *Jade*," he said to me smiling as we walked away. Giving me an exaggerated finger wave. I thought he was funny, and I smiled back. Then we left.

After another thirty minutes of window-shopping, we

decided to visit the food court and grab a slice of pizza. It was there that one of my neighbors, Mrs. Sanchez, approached our table while we were eating. It wasn't uncommon to see people from the neighborhood at the mall, so I didn't think anything of it at first.

"Jade?"

"Oh hi, Mrs. Sanchez."

"Hey, babe. Uh, when was the last time you checked in at home?"

"Not since earlier this morning, why?"

"Well, hun, I think your dad's been at it again."

"Really?"

I was so embarrassed. I could have crawled under the table. My girlfriends knew nothing about my shitty life at home. Now they were getting an ear full.

"Yeah, so your sister is at Linda O'Neal's house. You may want to get home. I think she's a little freaked out."

"Thanks, Mrs. Sanchez. I'll get home right now."

"Do you need a ride? I just have to grab something out of Macy's and then I'll be ready to go."

"Thank you anyway, but I'm fine."

Most of my teenage moments were cut short and ruined because of my father. Mall visits. Phone calls. Hanging with friends. And forget about boys. Even when we were very little my father wouldn't have ever won any sort of dad-of-the-year award, but he was all my little sister Jana and I knew, so to us he was like Superman and Spiderman rolled into one. What we were too young to realize back then was that my mother was the glue that held our little family together, and once she died, our fractured unit fell completely apart.

My father always had a drinking problem, way before my mother's death, but she knew how to shelter us from it. Protecting us from his tantrums. Shielding us from embarrassing moments. Making excuses for him that little girls believed. Holding the family together.

She went to work.

She paid the bills.

She checked the homework.

She talked to the teachers.

She cooked the meals.

She cleaned the house.

She did every damn thing. So when she died quickly and ruthlessly from ovarian cancer, needless to say, everything fell completely apart in our home. My father's drinking dramatically increased and with it so did his tantrums and his black outs.

He usually got *really* drunk Friday nights after work, which is why I would never make plans on Fridays, but then he'd sleep in most of the day Saturday. So that's why I thought it would be safe to hang out at the mall for a couple of hours during the early day.

Usually on a Saturday, he'd be in bed sleeping it off, and my sister would be on the computer looking at Disney shows for half of the morning, so I figured no one would even miss me for a couple of hours. I just wanted to hang with my girlfriends and be a normal teenager for once. Not stay in the house all day to keep an eye on him and my sister. I hated that that's what my life had become. I never asked for the responsibility. I resented that it had been thrust upon me. And I missed my mother desperately.

It was just my luck that when I let my guard down, for just a moment, my father had to go and have another tantrum. Tossing furniture around the living room like a lunatic. Then passing out on the couch with the front door open, but the screen door locked, so that the whole block could peep in and see him passed out in his underwear.

Luckily Jana knew the routine. *When Daddy starts acting*

like a crazy person, run downstairs and get out of the house through the basement door. Then off to one of the neighbors.

We verbally ran through it a million times with each other, and we actually had to do it together several times, but she never had to get out alone. So not only was I pissed that my father caused all this drama and embarrassment, and that I wasn't there to protect my little sister, but now my friends were looking at me as if I was the most pitiful person on the planet. Mrs. Sanchez said all of this in front them as if it was common knowledge that I was the daughter of the neighborhood drunk. As far as I knew, they didn't know anything about my life at home. At least that's what I liked to believe back then.

I remember throwing on my suit of bulletproof emotional armor and acting like what she said didn't faze me one iota. The last thing I needed was this story getting back to school. I didn't want pity, I didn't want anyone's intervention, and I didn't want advice. I just wanted to be left alone to handle it myself.

"Um, guess I better head home early." I remember saying casually as I took another bite of pizza.

"Of course, girl."

"Buses run every fifteen minutes right?"

"Yep. There will be another one any minute."

"Cool."

Then *he* came over.

If I could go back and tell my fifteen-year-old self to run like hell, I would. I should have gotten up from that table and taken the bus, but I didn't.

"I'll take you home," Tyson said.

I stared at him quietly, not knowing what to say. First of all, he was older. If he was driving, he was too old for me. Secondly, I knew better than to take a ride from some strange guy, but I wanted to get to Jana. Ms. O'Neal would no doubt be pumping her for information about our father, and our home life, and she was only eleven. She would eventually crack under the pressure. And if that happened, the entire neighborhood was going to know what was going in our house. Perfect way for child protective services to get in our business, and neither of us wanted that.

"Don't you have a Christmas display to fix?" My friend Tyra asked him with a tinge of teenage sarcasm.

"I just got off work, and it sounds like your girl here needs to get home sooner rather than later."

He looked at me. "So what's up? You need a ride?"

"Okay," I blurted out in response. Somewhat tongue-tied. Not really thinking about the consequences of my actions. I was blinded by my budding teenage hormones plus a strong desire to get home to my sister.

Even in work attire, Tyson looked liked he just completed an X-Games competition. Motor biking. Skateboarding. Extreme skiing. He just had that look. A slim but fit build. Assorted tattoos. A bleached blond faux Mohawk. Not to mention that he had to be three or four years older than me. A total turn on for a fifteen-year-old girl looking for any excuse to rebel against her father. Her life.

Back then I didn't have a cell phone. That was a luxury that we couldn't afford. So I promised my friends that I would email them when I got in the house. Knowing good and well it was probably likely that I wouldn't be able to send them much of anything. When my father had a tantrum, he tended to gravitate towards the electronics, and we only had one old desktop computer. My mother's. Although I prayed that it had been spared his wrath.

As soon as we got into the car, Tyson asked me if I needed a little something to relax before I dealt with my father. I wasn't exactly sure what he meant by that, but I assumed it was an alcoholic drink. That's what my father said on many occasions when he poured himself a scotch.

"*I just need something to relax, peanut.*" My father's nickname for me.

"I don't drink," I told Tyson firmly.

"I don't mean alcohol. I've got a little Oxy."

"What's that?"

"A pain reliever. It's prescribed by doctors. Totally safe. It'll give you a nice buzz, so you won't be as stressed out."

"I don't know—"

"Here, you can have one and see what it's like. I take them after work and on the weekends to wind down instead of getting all pissy on alcohol. Plus most girls I know like them, because there's no calories."

I still wasn't sold.

Not until he dangled it in front of me then took it away.

"Never mind. You might not be ready—"

"No," I stupidly said. "I want to try it." Imploring with my eyes for him to give me another chance. To give me the OxyContin. "Let me just deal with my dad and my sister first," I said in an effort to stall actually taking the thing. "I don't want to talk to them high."

I remember Tyson giving me a strange look after that. As if he was impressed with my mature decision making, but at the same time irritated with the fact that I made those choices.

What I didn't realize at the time was that this very part of my personality, my maturity beyond my years and my ability to rise to a stressful occasion without the need to numb myself, is what Tyson grew to resent. My strengths were his weaknesses, and he hated me for it. It was the part of me that he spent years trying to suffocate and annihilate. And the terrifying part was that he almost succeeded.

CAMDEN

It's been a couple of days and I haven't seen or talked to Jade. Supposedly she's been doing some leftover work for Roman that she needed to finish up before devoting herself to the club and our arrangement, but my guess is that's just an excuse. She's definitely ducking me.

The little gumball never showed up at the mini-mart the other night, and after waiting for an extra twenty minutes, I spun around to her house to look for her, but she wasn't there. I knew she was lying to me. Something is definitely going on. Jade's one fault is that she can't really lie worth a damn. So I'm assuming to avoid the embarrassment of having to try, she's decided to duck and dodge me. Hoping that eventually I'll let it go. And I would have, until Cutter called.

"You may want to get over here."

"Why? I thought we agreed that you'd handle the club tonight."

Funny how I have less of a desire to be at Lotus if Jade isn't there for me to watch.

"If you want Marco to take your sloppy drunk munchkin home then okay."

"What the fuck are you talking about, Cutter?"

"I'm saying that Jade is here at the club, plastered, and she's all over Marco."

"Drunk?!"

"Totally and all over Rico Suave."

"Well take her ass home then!"

"When has Jade ever done anything that she doesn't want to do? And trust me, she doesn't want me to take her home. She wants Marco to—"

"Shut your damn mouth. I'll be there in fifteen. Keep her there."

Cutter laughs out loud. "All right, brother. That I can do."

When I arrive to Lotus, I practically run out of the car and into the club like it's on fire. I throw the side door open, and charge my way angrily towards the bar like I'm thirteen years old again, and someone has stolen my bike.

I don't see my brother anywhere, but I definitely see that douche, Marco. He's behind the bar closing out the register while telling some sort of story to Jade, and she's sitting at the bar hanging onto his every word. Fucking laughing. Hysterically. As if he's some celebrity comedian doing a stand up routine on HBO. Like he's the funniest jackass on the planet.

I could strangle them both. I'd be totally fine with it. Hell, I almost killed a few people speeding on the expressway to get over here. So what're two more bodies?

When Marco notices my arrival he doesn't even flinch. Cocky bastard. In fact, my eyes better be playing tricks on me, because I swear he may have even smirked at me.

"Let's go," I command as I firmly pull on Jade's upper arm.

"Kinggg Kongg." Jade smiles and slurs when she sees me. There's something about her saying a nickname that I usually despise tonight which is making my dick brick hard.

"That's right, it's me. Let's go."

"Where are we going?" She giggles. "Marco was telling me the funniest story *everrr*. He said he could finish the story over pancakes."

"Did he now?"

I stare the little shit down.

"Pancakes are the best thing for soaking up liquor," he says in what I know now to be a Cuban accent that he turns on and off at will.

"Oh would you stop with that fake fucking accent already," I grumble.

He laughs at me as I bend down in front of Jade.

"Get on," I command. "I'll make you pancakes."

"Ooh, a piggyback ride!" she exclaims. "Bye, Marco. We'll finish the story another time."

Oh no the fuck you won't.

I flinch when Jade drunkenly slaps the side of my head. "Giddy up, Trigger!" She's wearing some sort of heavy ring on her right hand and it stung like hell, but I have to admit, that there's something about a drunk Jade that is amusing. She's a little silly, a lot more playful, and kind of cute.

"Wrap your arms around my neck and stop playing around." I fuss with her to keep from grinning. Plus I don't want her to fall and break her neck. I don't think I've ever seen Jade this sloshed.

"Don't forget her phone," Marco says.

Dammit, my hands are full of ... ass.

"Slide it in her back pocket and watch your hands. No wait. Where's Cutter?"

"I think you might even have Roman beat with this overprotective schtick of yours. I'm just going to slide her phone in her jeans like so." He slides her iPhone in her back pocket with two fingers in an exaggerated manner. "See? I didn't touch a thing."

Jade giggles in my ear. The sound totally redirects me from plopping her ass on the ground, and reaching across the bar to smack the only employee in the place with built in job security. Marco is the only employee left who worked at Lotus before we took it over. We keep his disrespectful ass around only because of that. That and the fact that he's a big draw for a lot of the women who patronize the club. They love his fake accent, his abnormally white teeth, and spending lots of money at the bar as long as he's working. That's his only saving grace.

"Good thing I didn't wear my leggings today huh, King Kong?"

"Shut up, Jade, and stop wiggling around back there."

I can feel her hardened nipples rubbing against my back, and it's making my dick grow even harder.

"Oh yes, sir! All hail the king—"

That mouth.

I would love for her to say all of that shit to me on all fours.

"The king is coming! So let it be written, so let it be done!"

She shows no signs of stopping her chain of corny Kingisms.

"God save the king!"

This girl's going to be the death of me.

Believe it or not this is my first time inside of Jade's apartment building, and as I look around, I spot a hundred different security breaches that I don't like. The *supposed*

secure front door to her building isn't locked. There's only one working elevator. The postman has left packages for the tenants on the front desk for anyone to grab. Hell, she's practically living in a college dormitory. No wait, a dorm would have better security than this.

"Has Roman ever been here?" I can't believe that he would ever cosign her living in a place like this.

"When I first moved in."

"Years ago?"

"Yeppppers."

"Why hasn't he been back?"

"The same reason why you haven't been here. No need for you to. I come to you guys."

True. I guess the place must have gone down hill since she first moved in.

"You never thought about moving? I know we pay you enough money to live somewhere better than this. Somewhere with a doorman and decent security."

I give her another piggyback ride inside the building to the elevator. She seems to be feeling dizzier.

"Nope, I like it here. Am I getting heavy?" she asks as we slowly move inside of her rickety elevator to the fifth floor. "You keep bobbing around like a buoy."

I laugh. "Actually I'm not bobbing around. That's your liquor soaked head playing tricks on you."

"Nah, admit it. I'm getting heavy."

"Jade, you weigh a hundred pounds soaking wet."

"Actually I weigh a lot more than that. It's all muscle though. Ryan works me hard. Can you feel how toned my glutes are now?"

"Who the hell is Ryan?"

"My personal trainer, silllly," she slurs. "You don't know anything about me."

"I know all the important stuff."

"You don't know shiznit."

"I know how to make you scream when you come," I assert. Finally shutting her right the hell up.

We finally arrive to her floor.

"Apartment five thirteen right?"

"You don't know my apartment number either? What kind of tracker are you?"

She sounds almost offended.

"What are you talking about?"

"You investigate everyone. What about me? Didn't you track me to Baltimore?"

" I followed you to the harbor, yes, but you're not a client, Jade. There was no need to investigate you. "

"Because my life is soooo boring to you?"

They say liquor acts as a truth serum. So I'm wondering, is that what she really thinks about her life and herself? That she's boring?

She's anything but.

"Are you saying that you are boring or that you're bored with your life?"

"My life is so *not* boring." She starts to laugh uncontrollably. "I wish it was."

I think I'm missing the joke.

"What made you drink like this tonight, Jade? Did something happen?"

"No."

"Why didn't you show up at the mini-mart the other day? You had me waiting for a long time."

"Sorry."

She's still fucking laughing.

"Where's your key?" I ask in exasperation. Fed up with trying to grill someone who's clearly too inebriated to answer.

"I dunno."

"Listen, drunky, if you want those pancakes we're going to need the key to open the door. Where is it?"

"Search me!" she says playfully as she throws her arms up. Almost falling back in the process.

"Will you hold on!" I order.

"Can't your bad ass just kick the door down or make another key? Like that MacGyver guy. Out of a gum wrapper and glue or something? You're smart like that."

She continues with her drunken laughter, but now she's rubbing my head with one of her hands, while holding onto my neck with the other. It feels incredible. If she wasn't so damn plastered, I'd slide her around to the front of me and grind her pretty ass against this wall.

"You're hair is so soft. You're like a puppy." She giggles. "We're not allowed to have dogs in this building."

I'm not sure that I like being compared to a dog, but I can't help but laugh at her drunken words. Normally Jade has to be "on" all the time. Working for us. Working a client. Her guard up. Her tough girl armor on. It's nice to see her let her hair down a little. Plus it feels kind of good that she thinks I'm a resourceful badass. Calling me MacGyver is a pretty high compliment in my book.

"I think it will be easier if we use a key," I tell her. Then I place her gently down on the floor next to the door.

"I think I left them at the club. Oh wait," she drunk whispers while pointing her finger in a downward motion. "I keep a spare key under the mat."

A key under the welcome mat of her front door? Does she want to get robbed or raped? Sure enough I lift up the mat, and there's an oversized, pink key with Hello Kitty on it underneath. This girl never ceases to surprise me.

"Are you insane? Has anything that we do for a living rubbed off on you at all?"

"Heck, yes! I'm paranoid all the time because of you guys."

"Clearly not enough if you're leaving keys under mats."

"Don't you see? I'm a genius." She's whispering again. Although I'm not really sure why, because there's no one within earshot distance of us, but it's the most adorable thing ever. "It's the most obvious place to hide it. That's why no one would ever think to look there."

The strong smell of Grey Goose that is emanating from Jade's pores reminds me exactly of why her reasoning is so ass backwards right now. How many vodka and pineapples did that lothario serve her? Me and him are definitely going to have words.

"You sound stupid," I chastise. "Come on and stand up."

I help her up onto her feet.

"Pfft," she mutters.

After walking Jade inside of her apartment, I slide her key in my back pocket for safe keeping and decidedly look around. She lives in a tight one-bedroom apartment. It's small, but the perfect size for her, and I like that the walls are painted with soft buttery colors that make the space feel warm and cozy. A definite contrast to Jade's edgy personality.

"Where's the bedroom?"

"That door." She points as her lids start to droop and fade into unconsciousness.

I scoop her up in my arms, before she completely falls on her face, and carry her to the room. Kicking open the door that was slightly ajar, I'm intrigued to find a large eleven-by-twenty-inch matted photograph prominently displayed on a wall above a vintage looking wood dresser. It's one of the only personal artifacts that I've seen in the house so far that reveals something about Jade that I didn't know.

The photo is a professional shot, like one of those ones you take at Sears. It looks like it's a picture of a very young Jade, another baby girl, and a woman whom they both look very much like but in different ways. Jade has the woman's eyes and freckles. The baby has her nose and mouth. All three of them are dressed in white tops and denim bottoms. Cute.

When Jade finally passes out, she sprawls across her queen-sized bed topped with sheets covered in small blue and yellow flowers and a tufted white comforter. When she's quiet like this, it gives me a moment to truly appreciate her beauty. She usually wears her hair pulled back off of her face, but seeing it splayed all over her pillow makes her look even sexier than she usually does. Her skin is blemish free and glowing. I think I even spot a couple of freckles on her face now that a lot of her makeup has worn off. She really is a striking woman wrapped in the tiniest, sexiest packaging ever.

I take my time stripping her of her clothing. It's been a while since I've seen what's underneath, and I'm damn near as excited as a child would be unwrapping his favorite toy under the Christmas tree. I think about how close I came to choking the bartender as I gaze at her. I'm possessive. I don't like other kids playing with my toys.

I untie and pull her favorite pair of converse off, placing them neatly by the bed. After removing her footie socks, I notice that her small feet and slender toes are painted a soft, petal pink. I lift one of her feet, cradling it in my hands. Carefully examining each and every toe. I'm starting to think that Jade secretly loves the color pink. First the pink spare key under the mat and now her pink painted toes. I'm interested by this, because it's been my experience that women who favor the color are very *girly* and Jade isn't.

She despises it when women talk about how "hot" a ball player is, because she takes her sports very seriously and cares more about their stats then their abs. She usually wears dark sweats, leggings or jeans—no dresses, no pastels. She only wears boots or sneakers—no heels. She never carries a handbag. Instead preferring to slide her phone in her back pocket, or the ankle of her boots, or inside of her bra. I think she keeps money and a credit card in the same hiding places too.

And while she is a woman of small stature, she isn't the least bit fragile. Jade's hills and valleys are all defined by strong, lean muscle where it counts and soft pliant flesh where it matters most. Most women are intimidated by her strong will and caustic mouth upon first meeting her. Some men too. But all of this is what makes her unique, and special, and sexy—especially to me.

Jade's feet are resting on my lap, and now that they're totally exposed to the air, she sleepily stretches them by flexing and pointing her toes. Inadvertently rubbing them against my cock and contributing to it's thickening inside of my pants.

I do my best to ignore that and start unzipping her jeans. They have to be the tightest pair of jeans ever made. I'm going to have to use a bit of force to get them down, and remember to make her go shopping for clothes that fucking fit next week. I lift her hips up with one hand and start tugging the jeans side to side, working them down her hips with my other hand. Once I get her jeans partially down, all I see and feel is warm, lush, velvety bare skin. She has no panties on, and she's freshly waxed.

Fuck.

I violently rub my face with my palm.

Another big mistake.

I can smell her on my fingers, and my balls start to tighten.

I try giving myself an internal pep talk. *What's the big deal? You've tasted her already. Just put her to bed and get out of here. Stop acting so fucking horny.*

So I keep going. I promptly tuck her legs and bare bottom under the covers, and then move on to her top half. Pulling her black cropped sweater up and over her head and quickly realizing why I felt her nipples earlier.

No bra.

What does this woman have against underwear?

Fucking hell, they're even better than I remembered. She has a pair of the most beautiful tits I've ever seen in my life. They look heavy and soft, the shape of teardrops, and her large areolas and nipples serve as perfect bull's-eye points ... for my mouth.

I'm like a starving man in a buffet line as I rake my eyes over them again and again. I want to stay up all night gawking at her, then wait for her to wake up, so I can eat her thoroughly for breakfast. Literally. But as if he could sense I was venturing into dangerous territory, a text from Cutter snaps me out of my lust filled daze. I take a couple of deep breaths of common sense, pull the covers completely up to her neck, and check my phone.

Cutter: Whatcha doing:)
    Me: Nothing.
    Cutter: Where's our drunken little brat?
    Me: Where did you go? I told you to keep her there.
    Cutter: And I did.
    Me: You left.
    Cutter: You didn't say I had to stay. I took care of it, then I rolled out.
    Me: You left her with the very person I was trying to protect her from!
    Cutter: Isn't she safe and sound?
    Me: No thanks to you.
    Cutter: Are you still with her?

Me: Why are you so curious after the fact?

Cutter: Just making sure she's okay.

Me: I'm at her apartment, but I'm about to leave. She's passed out.

Cutter: Bet you're pissed about that:)

Me: Not now, assface.

Jade turns over on her side and starts to breathe heavily. A few stray hairs fall over her face. I move them out of the way, slowly stroking them back into place. I touch her a little longer than necessary when I hear her start to almost purr.

"Cam?" she calls out groggily. "I should tell you—"

"Tell me what, itty bitty?" I ask as I reluctantly pull my hand away from her face. Happier than I should be that she's called out for me by name.

She turns on her opposite side, trying to adjust herself in a more comfortable position. The covers slide down again, exposing her breasts. I have a strong urge to continue touching her. Maybe even stroke her bare pussy a few times to make her come real quickly. I'd really be doing her a favor, right? That will absolutely help her relax and put her into a nice deep sleep. Maybe I will do just that if these sheets slide down just a wee bit farther ...

"Cam?"

"Yes, Jade?" I ask with a dry mouth and a hard dick.

"I gotta ... I gotta throw up."

Ugh, maybe not tonight.

JADE

Sooo, I'm not handling this news about Tyson's brother well at all. After revealing himself to me, the smart thing for me to do would have been to tell Camden immediately. He was literally a three-minute drive away that night. Waiting for me at the mini-mart. He probably would have shoved the prick into the trunk of the car, and continued with our excursion to the mall without even batting an eyelash. Problem solved. Yet I didn't do the *smart* thing.

It's actually quite hypocritical the way I've decided to handle this unwelcomed visitor, especially because of how I've busted Elizabeth's balls in the past about trust, honesty, and keeping shit from Roman. Now I'm doing the same exact thing.

It's a little bit of a different situation though, because I'm not sleeping with anyone like she is, but if I'm honest with myself, I know that's just an excuse to justify my actions. I haven't said anything yet, because Tyson is a chapter of my life that I've never really completely closed the book on, and now there's this asshole sitting outside my apartment who possibly has answers as well as access to achieving that.

I figured that after finding my face half beaten all those years ago, that Roman would give Tyson a beat down that would scare him away for a good while. Long enough for me to move out of the apartment and for my bruises to heal. I never actually believed that Tyson would completely disappear from my life though. I thought he'd be a thorn in my side for a very long time, but just like Roman promised, he made it so that Tyson never returned to bother me again. And I never asked about him again.

While the sane part of my brain knew that Roman's favor ended up being the best gift ever given to me, a small part of me always felt conflicted. Not because I wanted Tyson back, but because I didn't get the closure that I truly needed.

That one last soliloquy.

I didn't get to stand on my pedestal and tell Tyson about all of the things he did over the years that hurt or pissed me off. I didn't get to tell him how excited I was to move on with the rest of my life without him in it. I didn't get to brag about all the new guys I planned on meeting and sleeping with. I didn't get to say any last parting words, like "fuck you." And finally—I wasn't the one to actually end the relationship, Roman was, and I've always regretted that. I should have been the one to do it.

That's a lot of crap for one person to carry around, but for the last few years, I've managed to bury much of it with nonstop work and plenty of noncommittal sex, but the arrival of Tyson's brother is forcing those bothersome feelings to resurface. So to cope, I've recently been turning to my spirit of choice lately—vodka.

Lots and lots of vodka.

My father would be proud.

"You want a drink?" I offer my stalker through my bedroom window. Showing him my glass of vodka and pineapple over ice. It's actually a rhetorical question, but I'm slightly interested as to how he'll respond.

From my vantage point, he seems to be eating chicken strips and fries inside of his car with the window down. If he really is Tyson's brother it's amazing how completely different they are from each other. Other than the similar tone of their voices, there's a big difference in their stature, coloring, and mannerisms including the fact that this guy doesn't say much. Tyson was always talking. Talking shit.

He cracks a smile at my disingenuous offer, and watches me carefully as he pops another fry into his mouth. Over the last few days or so since he's revealed himself, you could say that the two of us have been having this strange standoff. I'm waiting for him to leave on his own, and I guess he's waiting for me to force his hand and make him leave. Neither of us budging.

I may be dumb, but I ain't stupid. Interrogating him about Tyson isn't going to make me feel better. It will only open up a ton of old wounds. Yet on the other hand, I'm just not ready to be the reason this guy ends up in the emergency room with a cracked jaw, because that's what will happen if I tell Camden, Cutter or Roman. That's why it would be best all around if I'd just come home one day and he's already gone.

I'm on my second cocktail of the evening, and I haven't even left my apartment yet. The liquid gold is doing its job by soothing my frayed nerves, but I better slow down. Not only is it pathetic and dangerous to start the habit of drinking alone, but I have to go to work at the club, and Camden will be watching.

He hasn't said anything yet, but I know that he wants to ask the questions. Where did I go when I didn't show up at the mini-mart? Why was I so drunk the other night that he had to escort me home? These are not things that are normal for me. I don't just stand people up, and I definitely don't get pissy drunk. Sooner or later he's going to want an explanation.

I brush my teeth and gargle twice to eliminate any traces of vodka on my breath. The ritual painfully reminds me of flashes of my childhood. My father would spend a lot of time in the only bathroom in the house, brushing his teeth and gargling with Listerine before greeting my mother hello. As if she had no clue that he just stumbled inside the house from the corner bar he frequented after work. Am I turning into my father? God, I hope not.

I'm not tipsy, but feeling relaxed when I leave my apartment, so I decide to cross the street and confront my unwanted guest. I stand in front of the driver's side window of his car, with my hands on my hips, popping a stick of gum in my mouth like it's a steak dinner. He seems to be finished with his food and is sitting in the car, with the window now up, chair tilted back, and texting someone on his cell phone. He doesn't acknowledge me at first, but I knock on the window and begin talking anyway.

"Hey, I'm leaving. You can go now," I say loudly enough so that he can hear me through the window. Shooing him with my hands.

"We should talk," he announces after rolling the window partially down.

"Umm, no," I respond sarcastically.

"Then I think I'll stay in front of your building a little while longer."

"How long? You're really starting to piss me off."

"When you're ready to talk. I'll leave."

"I already know what you want to say."

"What do you think I'm going to say?"

"Knowing Tyson it has something to do with money, but

you can tell him that I don't have any, and even if I did I wouldn't give any to him. I haven't seen or heard from him in years, and I want to keep it that way. That's if you're really even his brother."

The guy doesn't respond but reaches into his glove compartment for something. My first reaction is to back away from the car just in case it's a gun, but he assures me it's not a weapon that he's reaching for.

"Relax, I'm just getting my ID."

He pulls out a semi-glossy looking, brown leather billfold wallet. Then retrieves a drivers license out of one of the credit card slots and hands it to me.

Chase Whitman
496 Bolier Road
Annapolis, Maryland

All types of synapses start firing up in my brain. It's probably not a coincidence that Tyson's brother is from Maryland, and I was sent on a wild goose chase there the night of the gala. I'm not ready to call him on it just yet. Not until I have more information.

"Okay so you have the same last name, but what's this supposed to prove?" I ask with a suspicious voice. "I dated Tyson for years and he never mentioned you."

"We have a dysfunctional family, like most people, but we've recently reconnected."

"How wonderful for you," I say snidely.

"I'm not here for money."

"I thought I was clear on not caring about why you're here. The only thing I'm interested in is you freeing up this parking space for people who actually live on this street, and if you don't leave in the next ten minutes, I'm calling the cops to help you along."

He raises an eyebrow. "I don't think you'll do that."

"And why the fuck not?"

"I'm not breaking any laws by parking here, and more importantly you and I both know calling the cops isn't your style. You would have done it by now if it was."

This asshole is calling my bluff.

"You are stalking me. Last time I checked stalking was against the law in every state of this great nation."

"So call the cops then."

Then before I can respond to his dare, the prick rolls up the window and puts a white hand towel over his face as if I've been dismissed. He called my bluff well. After years of dealing with a raging alcoholic and his erratic mood swings, I've been conditioned to not calling the police. Sticking my father into jail to sober up was never a good idea, because he would come home meaner than ever.

So he's right. I'm not going to call anyone. I'm not going to do anything. Not quite yet. Not until I figure out exactly who this Chase Whitman really is and what he wants with me. Especially because Tyson's involved.

I'm running late when I arrive at Lotus. I'm usually the first one to the club, to a meeting, to the gym, to anywhere that I need to be. But doing things out of character lately seems to be a running theme in my life right now. Fortunately everyone seems preoccupied with work, so they aren't paying much attention to the fact that the new manager, who's been missing in action, has finally shown up—late.

Marco is opening up the bar for the night, Cutter is troubleshooting an issue with the sound system, and the custodial staff is having a mini meeting in the far corner of the club. The person I truly want to avoid is nowhere in sight, and not parked in his usual perch on the second floor of the club keeping an eagle eye on everyone. In fact on my way in, one of our bouncers said that Camden has been working non-stop for hours in the office and hasn't popped his head out once. Perfect.

I'm told by staff that the girl, Leah, who usually collects money at the door during the week called out. Something about her kid having the flu, so it looks like it will be my job to handle the door for the evening. That's a big part of my job for the boys. I fill in wherever necessary, because I know how to practically do everyone's job.

It's not time for me to start working the door yet, so I decide to sit at the bar and have a drink. I rationalize to myself that it's the only way to mask the fact that I've already had two others. I'm ironically sipping on my vodka and pineapple when the club's liquor distributor pops in for a visit.

Patrick is a good guy. Funny, respectful, and kind of flirty. We usually talk for a good while on the phone when I place my wine and spirits order for the bar every month, but it's nice to see him in person. Especially because he isn't that bad to look at. Average height, stocky build, kind eyes. He'll be a great distraction for me tonight. Anything to keep my mind off of Tyson's brother, as well as the King I've been avoiding for days.

"Well hello, Miss Barlow."

"Hi to you too, Pat."

"Are you working hard tonight or hardly working?"

"Unfortunately I have to work the door tonight. Not my favorite job. Every woman in the tri-state area thinks they should get in free if they've slept with one of the owners." I laugh. "You should see their reactions when I tell them that they have to pay twenty-five bucks to get in, but we'd never turn a profit if I didn't charge them all."

Patrick laughs. He always thinks whatever I say is funny, which is nice.

"Aww, damn. I thought we'd finally get a chance to dance and party in here tonight. I don't have to work tomorrow."

"Well you should absolutely stay. There will be plenty of gorgeous women in here tonight for you to charm with those eyes of yours."

Although they're kind looking, Patrick actually has a set of very average brown eyes, but everyone likes to be paid a compliment. Plus I think my flirting helps with the rock bottom wholesale price he gives us for our bottles.

"Yet I only want to dance with you."

"Awww, aren't you sweet."

"What are you drinking? You want another?"

"Grey Goose and pineapple, and no, maybe later."

"The good stuff," he says referring to my choice of vodka.

"Yep, you want to taste?"

I hold the glass up to his lips for him to take a sip. He stares at me like a horny middle school boy while he takes a small gulp of my drink. I'm pretty sure he feels that he's laid enough groundwork with me over the last few months to finally get me into bed and not feel guilty about it. I can tell that's the kind of guy Patrick is. Someone who doesn't have ass just handed to him. He has to work for it, and I appreciate a hard worker. They always try their best in bed. Maybe he'd be just the thing to make me forget about my incredible one-night stand I had with Camden. In fact, maybe Patrick could help distract me over the next thirty days.

I smile while Patrick takes a swallow, and then I allow him the honor of watching me take another sip of the drink in the same exact place where his lips just were. My eyes locked on his. Then I lick my lips afterwards for effect. When he tries to adjust his dick without me seeing, I grin to myself.

Works every single time.

"So are you staying?" I ask seductively already knowing the answer.

"I'll be right here when you're finished."

I turn the corner of my lips up.

"Want another sip?"

CAMDEN

I've spent the better part of my afternoon digging around two year's worth of some poor sap's phone records. He's been a busy boy. Calling people he had no business calling. Proof that he's been double crossing one of our clients. Which is great news for us. This will be an easy couple of grand in our pocket.

I was just finishing up when Cutter comes barreling into the office like he always does. He never enters a room quietly. It's not in his DNA. He always busts in, rarely knocking, and announcing himself as if nobody in the room knows who the hell he is. He spares me the King's greeting this time, but ends up telling me something that I want to hear even less.

"Patrick is here."

"All right already! Why do you always have to barge in here like the goddamn cops. I swear I'm going to accidentally put a bullet in your chest one day if you don't learn how to enter a room like a normal person."

"You need to see someone about all that pent up anxiety

of yours, big brother. When's the last time you got laid? I know just the spot we can go to after work." He grins.

Cutter knows good and well that I'm not going to go to some broken down, dirty, titty bar to look for some ass. We have plenty to choose from right here, and it sure as hell smells better. Not to mention that I only seem to want one ass in particular lately, and I haven't had a taste of the shit in months. My patience is wearing thin. I've never waited so patiently for a woman in my life.

"Didn't you get your dick burned twice from messing with the girls in that place? No, thank you. I pass on that penicillin resistant pussy. And what does Patrick want? I don't have time to shoot the shit with him. I'm busy. You handle it."

"He's not here for you or me."

"So what are you telling me for then? Jade put the liquor order in last week. The check cleared. What could he possibly want?"

I start reading emails.

"I think he may be *double checking* the order with her specifically."

I raise my head.

"Double checking a monthly order in person?"

"Eh, I think the little liquor pusher may have a hard on for our girl."

The fuck.

All I can see in my head are wretched visions of Jade on her knees in front of creepy ass Patrick in the middle of my dance floor, because that is something else nerve wracking about this woman ... most men are *very* attracted to her, and she does very little to discourage it.

She has a taut, flat stomach, curvy hips, teardrop breasts, and a pair of sexy ass lips. Not to mention that she often uses her sexuality to her advantage. She is a big ass flirt by nature and depending on her mood, she will back up all that flirting with actual fucking. The kind that most men dream about. Hot, no strings attached, no drama, no staying the night, fucking with a woman small enough to flip into almost any position imaginable.

I'm the first to admit that Rome, Cutter and I have played a part in promoting some of that behavior. Having her flirt with a dickhead or two to get some information or to act as a distraction. Men are so predictable and fall for that shit every time, but we have *never* asked her to fuck anyone; and now I'm even starting to second guess our strategy of suggesting she do anything flirty at all. It's backfiring on my ass. Big time.

"I'll be right back," I tell my brother.

The club is only filled with a few employees, because it's still early. Jade is seated at the bar with a drink in her hand and playing with a cocktail napkin. Patrick is leaning against the bar counter, towering over her, while apparently talking shit in her ear. Even though she's only wearing a pair of skintight jeans and a basic black tank top, she exudes effortless sex appeal.

But Patrick is not a mark.

We don't need any information extracted from him. We don't need him for shit, but to deliver our liquor order on time. So it's plain as day that this is not a business call. This is for pleasure. Which is becoming particularly obvious, after I watch Jade giggle like a schoolgirl at something lame he has no doubt just said in her ear. Real laughter. The kind where she shuts her eyes and grabs his arm to keep herself from falling over in rip fucking roaring laughter.

She actually likes this underachiever, and the realization of that sends an irrational signal to my brain that makes all the hairs on the back of my neck rise up. I want to take the ballpoint pen that's in my hand and drive it into the gut of my liquor distributor. I actually want to hurt him, *badly*.

Most eyes are on me as I make my way down the spiral staircase and approach the two of them. One of my part-timers, Joan, is behind the bar checking inventory and washing wine glasses. I sit down at the bar in front of her and on a stool, which is on the other side of Jade. The little vixen doesn't even attempt to turn her head to acknowledge me. That irks me even further.

"Pour me a scotch, Joan."

"Sure thing, King."

None of the club's employees call me by my first name. That's a privilege pretty much reserved for very close friends and family. Cutter hates it though, because they can only call one of us King to avoid confusion. Probably why he's always announcing himself when he walks into the room as "the king."

"Hey, King." Patrick gives me an unusually friendly greeting. It's instinctual between men. He already knows that I don't like what I'm seeing and is overcompensating. Slimy little fucker.

"What's up, Pat?" I give him a stiff head nod. "Is there a mix up with the order or something?"

"Naw, man." He chuckles uncomfortably. "I was in the area, so I thought I'd drop by to make sure Jade was umm ... happy with the delivery."

"Is that right." I stare so far down his throat I can see the asshole's tonsils. "Well it's nice to see that the staff at Bella Vargo Distributors takes customer service seriously. I'll have to give Paulie a call and talk you up."

Patrick takes a moment to think about what he is going to say next. It's actually kind of amusing. He knows me. He knows my reputation. And he's no idiot. He doesn't want to offend me, but he doesn't want Jade to think that he's a punk either. Which is too bad for him, because this thing is not going to end well for him.

"We do take it seriously, especially when we do business with customers we value."

He winks at Jade and when she smiles in return, I immediately feel my pulse quickening and adrenaline pumping through my veins. *What the fuck?* I feel like I'm in high school again. I want to drag him into the boy's locker room, and smash his head into one of the lockers.

It's obvious to me now. My attraction to Jade, and my feelings for her, have morphed into something bigger. Something possessive. Something inexplicably complicated. I recall how Roman warned me that I needed to handle her with kid gloves, when the warning actually should have been to make sure that I protected myself. She may possibly have the power to bring me to my knees, and the scariest part of it is that she has zero clue that she wields it.

I understand Roman's hesitance about my intentions though. Relationships are my kryptonite. I always have good intentions, but I don't do relationships well, and I don't do them for long. Not to mention that I seem to always hurt someone along the way, but if there's one thing I know for certain, it's that I don't want to hurt Jade.

"And we appreciate your business," *motherfucker*, "but I'm going to have to ask you to leave, so we can get ready to open. Jade's hasn't been to work in *days*, so she has some catching up to do. You know how it is in the club." I smirk after giving him his walking papers in the most polite way that I possibly can. My balls are going to start to shrivel into the size of marbles if I'm any nicer.

"I can come back later as a *paying* customer. Jade promised me a dance."

I know he didn't intend his words to come out the way that they did, and maybe I'm overreacting, but I think he just inadvertently said that he wanted to come back and pay Jade for some pussy.

"The fuck did you just say?" Cutter butts into the conversation challenging Patrick.

Oh good, I'm not nuts, Cutter heard it too.

"Pay to get inside of the club and then dance with Jade," Patrick responds as if he's been insulted. "Obviously."

"Not tonight, homeboy," Cutter says.

"She's busy," I say at the same time.

Patrick glares at the two of us, then leans over to Jade and whispers something in her ear.

"Okay," she grins. "I will."

My eyes angrily snap back to the little fucker's face, as I wonder to myself what the hell did he just get her to agree to? He gives her a slight peck on the cheek, and gives Cutter and I a head nod good-bye, and then he leaves. He's ballsy. I'll give him that much. Too bad I make a living out of cutting the balls off of motherfuckers.

"Are you drunk or just fucking crazy?" I ask as I move in dangerously close to her. Her warm breaths blowing against my neck. I can almost feel her heart trying to beat itself out of her chest.

"Hardly," she responds while gradually backing away from me.

I'm starting to enjoy that I make her nervous. The shit turns me on.

"Listen, I don't know what's going on with you, but I need you to stop getting drunk at my club. You probably gave Marco a pair of blue balls the other night when you were in here flirting with him. Then when I lugged your drunk ass home, you threw up all over yourself, and I had the distinct displeasure of cleaning it up. Aren't you even a little bit embarrassed?"

"Not even a little bit."

I sigh to myself. She always has to be a hard ass. I study Jade quietly for a moment. Her breathing. Her body language. I don't like what I'm seeing. She hasn't been herself lately. She's been running late or ditching work completely. She's been lying, and the other day she looked tired. Like she's sitting up all night worried about something.

"Is this agreement too much for you?"

"What?" She looks over at Cutter. Hoping that he's not eavesdropping but he is.

"Is our arrangement too much for you to handle? You're not acting like yourself."

"I don't know what you're talking about."

"It's been a week, and you haven't really been here."

"I told you. I had to finish up some things for Roman, but I'm here now Mr. King, ready and reporting for duty as requested."

I stare at her suspiciously not buying anything she's selling.

"I'm handing over the liquor orders to Marco starting next month," I tell her.

"For what," she protests. "I've been handling liquor for Lotus ever since we opened."

"Marco knows the bar better than anyone. He's the bar manager. It should be his job. That's what we pay him for."

"So what do I even need to come here for if you're going to take away every responsibility I have?"

"Stop being dramatic. You're the temporary manager of this club and you manage *us*. Those are your jobs. Not menial tasks like ordering inventory."

"Ordering liquor is a managerial task that occurs once a month. It's only a phone call."

"Exactly," Cutter chimes in from across the room. "Why was Patrick even here if it only requires a phone call?"

Jade whips her head between Cutter and me in

frustration and throw her hands up. "Because obviously I'm going to *fuck* him! Do you two imbeciles need me to spell it out for you?"

She really deserves to get her ass paddled for that comment. For her attitude. For her lying. In fact, my mouth starts to water at the very thought.

Jade in restraints.

Ass in the air.

Mine.

"You're not going to fuck the liquor guy. End of story. We have too good of an arrangement with the company for you to ruin it with your raging hormones," I say.

"Are you serious right now? You fuck a different woman every couple of days, and I can't get laid by a guy that we know, like, and trust."

"Who said I liked him? And I sure as shit never said I trusted him."

"I trust him!"

"Ha!"

"What does that mean? Are you insinuating that I don't have good judgment? Because that's awfully funny coming from you. The last woman who you *and* your brother over there fucked senseless hasn't stopped crank calling the club every night. She's got to be the dumbest woman on the planet, if she doesn't think that I don't know that it's her giggling in the background. That silly bitch has one ménage and loses her mind."

"That wasn't the last one," I say.

"What are you talking about?"

"That wasn't the last woman we fucked senseless."

I can hear Cutter chuckling softly across the room.

She rolls her eyes. "You're such a dick, Camden. You both are."

I'm pleased with the fact that I've left her with a very

interesting visual to stew over for the rest of the night. I actually haven't fucked anyone senseless since I was inside of her, but there's no need for her to know that ridiculous truth. She probably wouldn't believe it anyway. My brother and I notoriously have a voracious appetite when it comes to sex.

"And you're off liquor detail." I patronizingly tap the end of her nose with my finger. "End of story. Now go make sure our guest deejay has everything he needs before you start working the door. I need to finish something up in the back."

"Screw you."

Jade sticks her middle finger up at me, smiling as she walks off, and I laugh harder than I have in a long time. I haven't met a woman who has made me so angry, so interested, and so amused in a long time. Her smile makes me smile. Her laughter makes me laugh. She makes me *feel* something, and that's rare for an emotionally unavailable person like me, but I continue to run back Rome's words of warning.

Is gambling with years of friendship worth the risk?

CAMDEN

I wasn't that impressed when I first met Jade Barlow. Sure she had a pretty face, and interesting almond shaped eyes, but she was also really short. I mean super tiny. And I usually liked my women long and lean, not that I was trying to make her my woman. She had a big mouth too. Large. Kind of foul. And some of the shit that came out of it could cut you like a razor. I preferred a woman's mouth refined and soft and wrapped around my dick.

Not to mention that the day we met, her shirt was torn, her eye was turning a pinkish purple color, and she had a busted lip. She'd been fighting, which wasn't a total surprise, because like I said, she has a big mouth. People were bound to have the desire to punch it.

Then when my best friend and business partner Roman, the imbecile who decided that we were going to hire this hot mess, explained the particulars around this brawl of hers, my opinion of her grew even less favorable.

She had been fighting a man.

Her boyfriend.

Willingly.

And evidently she did this on a regular basis.

Jade was not the typical type of young woman you hear about who's being battered by her boyfriend. Frightened. Trapped. Alone. Girls who don't see a way out of the abusive relationships they find themselves in. That I can understand. I've seen it first hand, but Jade was different.

From what I was told about her over the years by Roman, she was smart and tough, but he left out one very important thing. She also craved drama. She liked the fighting. Probably because she thought it meant that her loser boyfriend loved her. She may have even picked a few of the fights. Looking for a battle. Which was even harder for my brain to compute, because it looked to me, like she was losing them all.

Big time.

It's that type of idiotic shit that I couldn't condone. She was damaged goods. A loose cannon. A liability. I certainly didn't want her handling any of our business. Our clients. Our money. Hell no. Roman's father and the owner of our business, Joseph, would never go for it either. Her life was too complicated, and there was no way in hell that any of us wanted that crazy to end up on our doorstep.

Crazy attracted police officers, and law enforcement meant questions. We certainly didn't need anyone questioning anything that the three of us were doing, because some of it wasn't legal. Actually most of it wasn't. I didn't care how many cops Roman's father may have had in his pocket. There were always cops that couldn't be bought. Cops that would be gunning for us if they got even a whiff of something illegal. And I sure as shit wasn't ever going to jail if I could help it. Not because of some crazy bitch.

"What the fuck, Jade?" Roman asked after knocking on her front door and noticing her bruised and disheveled appearance.

"I know what it looks like—"

118

"It looks like you got beat the fuck up."

"Really? Then you should see what the other guy looks like," she said in jest. At least I think it was a joke.

"Where is that motherfucker?" I rarely saw Roman become that genuinely pissed about other people's domestic clusterfucks, but he was officially mad. His anger seemed to cause a moment of worry to cross Jade's face. My question was who she was worried about. The boyfriend or herself.

"He's not here."

"You can't hide him from me forever."

"I'm not hiding him. He's just out. We needed some distance after our … altercation."

She pointed to me. "Is this him?" Looking me carefully up and down as if she was in any position to make an assessment about anything or anyone.

"Are you going to let us in?" Roman asked rhetorically.

"Yes, of course." She sounded flustered for a moment. "Come in."

It didn't take but a second to see why she was so hesitant to let us in. The place was trashed. The few pieces of bullshit furniture in the apartment had been tossed on their sides. Clothes were strewn around the room. Old dirty dishes were piled in the sink and on the counter. Some were even broken into pieces.

The mess in her house wasn't from one lover's quarrel. It was definitely cumulative. That's when I decided that if what I was seeing was any indicator of the cleanliness and organizational skills of the assistant we were there to hire, I was going to have to veto it. And my vote counted for two people, my brother and I, against Roman's one.

"Jade," Roman said practically seething as he looked around.

"I know, Roman, but—"

119

"This place looks like a goddamn meth lab. Where is he? I want to know right the fuck now. Is he getting high?"

"He doesn't do meth," she explained while looking over at me. As if I cared one way or another what her boyfriend's choice of drug was. The fact that he got high was all I needed to know.

Roman rephrased the question.

"Whatever the fuck it is. He's out buying it right now isn't he?"

"Maybe."

"With your money?"

"Probably," she answered solemnly.

"I can't let this stand anymore, Jade."

"I said I'd handle it."

"Look at your fucking face. This house. Do you honestly think you've got a handle on this situation?"

I noticed a crack in the tough girl's armor. She was embarrassed, she was in over head, and I was pretty sure she wanted to ask for help but didn't know how to. Especially with me, someone she just met, standing in the room.

I didn't know much about Jade, hadn't even really heard her name much, until Roman brought up the idea of hiring her. Roman wasn't a big sharer, but the little he did tell me was that while she hadn't grown up in our neighborhood, somehow the two of them met when she was a teenager. I never asked for the particulars, because I always assumed that she was just some girl that he may or may not have fucked back in the day. A blast from his past that he all of a sudden wanted to help out.

It was a hiring we debated for a couple of days because one: I didn't know her, and two because I didn't think we needed another person privy to the inner workings of our *complicated* business.

A trial run is what he countered.

I didn't have a good feeling about it though. Especially after what I had just witnessed. That drama queen needed an intervention not a job.

"Do you still want to work for us, Jade?" he asked her.

"Yes," she answered solemnly.

"Then it starts with you getting your shit straight. You can't work for me and live like this. Tomorrow you get up and look for another place. A place you don't tell the douchebag about. I'll take care of the security deposit and first month's rent. You can pay me back later."

"That's not going to work for me, Roman—"

That was it for me. I'd had enough at that point. She was turning down a very gracious one-way ticket out of loser land, and it made no sense to me. I had to jump in and stop that crazy train from traveling any further towards *this is fucking stupidville.*

"Are you insane?" I cocked my head to the side and questioned her.

"What the hell did you just say to me?" she asked with way too much attitude.

The balls on that chick.

"I said are you *insane.* Out of your mind. One fry short of a happy meal. You live with some sort of addict who beats on you, and you don't want to leave?"

"He doesn't beat on me. We argue. Things sometimes get out of hand. It happens to everyone."

"Happens to everyone? No, sweetheart, it doesn't. I've never hit a woman in my life," I countered. "I think Jerry Springer still has his talk show in syndication if you and your druggie want to send over a video submission, because you sound nuts."

"I have an exit plan, Mr. Need To Mind Your Own Fucking Business," she rolled her eyes. "I don't need anyone's help or anyone's judgment."

"Everybody has a plan until they get punched in the mouth."

"Cam—" Roman interrupted.

"No wait, I'm serious," I said in defense of my position. "First of all, we come to *her* house for a fucking job interview. Who the hell does that? She should have come to us. *The employers.* Then when we get here she's looking like a UFC fighter ... who lost by the way and lives in a crack den. And on top of all of that, she doesn't want any help to stop it?"

"Roman knows me, you don't. I would ask for help if I really needed it."

"Then you're a fucking idiot, because you really need it now."

If looks could kill, then I would have been shot right on the spot. She hated me, which was fine with me, because I didn't like her either; and I definitely didn't want her working for me.

"Jade, just do what I asked you to do this weekend," Roman ordered. "Call me when you're ready to finalize everything, and I'll bring a check over. Then report to work on Monday at my father's house. I'll text you the exact address."

"What about Tyson?"

"I'll take care of him. I met him once or twice. I remember what he looks like."

"But—"

"I'm going to help you, but just this one time. If you take that motherfucker back in after this, then you're on your own. No job. No help. No more contact. I don't do second chances, and I'm not friends with stupid people."

I scoffed out loud at that comment. As far as I was concerned she was the stupidest woman I had ever met.

She stared at both Roman and I silently but intensely.

Like a teapot warming to a slow boil. She was angry. Angry that she'd no doubt been exposed, called on her shit, and given a stern ultimatum. But I'm pretty sure that she was scared too, and being frightened was at least something I could understand.

I remember thinking, hoping, that perhaps Roman's friend wasn't a total idiot. That maybe she was trapped in her own cycle of self-sabotage and destructive behavior and needed a little push to get out.

"Do you want my help or not?" Roman demanded to know once and for all.

"I do," she said flatly and under her breath.

I could tell it pained her to say the words, but what I found even more remarkable was that she genuinely seemed to be worried that she'd lose Rome's friendship.

"I can't hear you."

"I do, dammit!"

"That's better. Now start packing up this place tonight."

"But—"

"He's not coming back tonight or the next. Don't worry about him."

"Okay," she exhaled in relief. "I don't feel like having another fight tonight."

That night Roman and I were both unusually quiet in the car until I broke the silence between us. I wasn't going to veto him about hiring Jade, because after what I witnessed between the two of them inside of that apartment, I knew it would be a lost cause. He cared about the little misfit toy for some reason, and he was determined to save her from herself. I was also starting to consider the possibility that he brought me there on purpose. To see for myself. To understand first hand why he wanted to give her the job, and why I shouldn't say no.

She needed us.

"Are you in love with that girl or something?" I asked. Knowing better than anyone that Roman had never slept with the same woman more than once, but it was the only rationale I could think of at the time for his bizarre level of patience with the tiny terror.

"No."

"Is she in love with you?"

"Ha! Not hardly."

"If I vetoed hiring her, would you accept my decision and move on?"

"Yes."

"But you'd be pissed."

He thought about his response for a moment.

"I'd understand why, but yeah, I'd be pissed."

"Joseph is never going to go for hiring her. Can you imagine if she gives him that same sort of attitude that she gave us just now? I didn't know women could also have Napoleon complexes. She's too damn small to act that bitchy."

"She's a little rough around the edges, but there's definitely something about you that brought out her claws today."

"Excuses. Excuses."

"Listen she knows how to tone it down when she needs to, and she will when she's around Joseph. We just caught her on a bad day."

"Make me understand, Rome. You knew we were probably going to find a mess when we got there. I would venture to guess that every day is a bad day in that house. So why this girl?"

"Simple. I trust her with my life, which means I trust her with yours."

~

We searched every hole in the wall that we knew of for Jade's boyfriend that night. We didn't find him. It wasn't until the next day that we located him, and it happened to be back home in their apartment. Sleeping across their dirty brown couch. Slobber practically dripping from the corner of his mouth. Jade wasn't at home, and hadn't called us either, so we assumed that he must have slithered in after she went out for the day.

He must not have been there long, because he was still high, and while he probably didn't feel much, it made me feel a whole lot better to punch him in the jaw until I drew blood. It didn't take much to scare the douchebag off. Roman and I beat his ass real good, threatened to do more if he ever came back around Jade again, and that was that. We never saw him again, and neither did she.

I also never saw her shed a tear over the dude either. In fact all I saw was a smart-mouthed, hyper-defensive, battle-worn girl turn into one of the most loyal, hard-working, assistants I'd ever seen. She metamorphosed practically overnight, and I'd been proven completely wrong about her.

Over time she became kind of the little sister Cutter and I never had. A girl who could hold her own, and keep our secrets close to the vest. Someone to help keep us on track, someone genuinely interested in seeing us succeed, and someone really adept at knowing what we needed or wanted even before we did. These were the many traits that ended up making Jade invaluable to us, and why the three of us anointed her as our "little sis." She took care of us. Very good care.

The problem now is that you don't fuck family, and think you can just go about the rest of your life like nothing happened. The shit doesn't work that way. Not when it's Jade. I wake up with morning wood thinking about her ass. I stare at her tits when she's talking to me about a client. I've started purposely saying things to make her laugh, because I think it's adorable how she squeezes her eyes tightly shut when she does. On Sundays I drop by Chickie and Pete's to watch the game with Cutter, and pray that she walks through the door too. And the biggest problem I'm facing? What to do with *the bodies* when a guy comes within a fifteen-foot radius of her.

Because they always do.

Like that asshole, Dallas.

JADE

When the boys saved me several years ago from the vicious cycle I was living in with Tyson, I had an epiphany. It took me some time, but one day I woke up, and it was like I'd been whacked with a hedge slammer. I realized that I'd been living a non-productive, toxic life, with a boy who just wasn't ever able to cope with becoming a man. I just didn't understand why I stayed around so long. What did that say about me?

My mother did her best to leave me with lots of life lessons before she passed. She didn't raise me to be a doormat, or a punching bag, or an idiot. Yet somehow, I allowed myself to become just that. All of that. What we didn't really talk much about, and I'd guess that's because I was so young when she became sick, was that relationships were complex. Men could build you up and tear you down all in one moment, or worse, slowly spread across little moments that occurred every single day. Until one day you looked up and you weren't the person who you were once were. Who you were supposed to be.

After living in a wasteland with Tyson, I felt a strong need to make up for lost time. I had spent much of my youth with him. Being smothered by him. Lost in him. The problem with moving forward was that I didn't know how to relate to other men. I knew the mechanics of sex, how to give pleasure, and how to receive it, because Tyson and I had plenty of it; but there were other things that I didn't know. So I made some mistakes over the post Tyson years.

I flirted with the wrong people. Slept with a few really bad apples. And the little bit of confidence I had left started to wane. So I created my list of rules. Hoping that creating some structure around who and how I dated would help. And for a time the rules definitely helped me keep things comfortable and casual, until I fucked up and broke every single one in a Baltimore hotel room.

How was I supposed to work with someone who knew my body better than my gynecologist? How was I supposed to go on with business as usual when he said all those depraved things in my ear that night? I prayed that someone would come along to help me forget Camden's touch, his body, his kiss, and how it felt when he was inside of me.

And then came a sliver of hope ... Dallas.

I was driving my mother's old Toyota Camry, a car that had seen better days, but that I didn't want to let go of, for sentimental reasons, when I met him. The car wouldn't start, and I was stuck in my worst nightmare—stalled on the Benjamin Franklin Bridge in the middle of rush hour.

I'd forgotten to renew my AAA membership, like an idiot, and I didn't want to call one of the guys. They were my last resort, because I knew if I did that I'd never hear the end of it about my "shitty car." They were dying for me to buy a new one.

It started to drizzle outside. Cars were whizzing by me. People drive a lot faster than you realize when you're just standing still by the side of a road. It was clear that people had places to go. Everyone wanted to get home, and no one seemed to want the bother of stopping in the rain to help me. No one but Dallas.

He was driving a black Acura sedan, and as soon as we made eye contact, he slowly pulled his car to the side on the slender shoulder of the bridge.

"Car won't start?" he asked after rolling down his window.

"I'm not sure what the problem is."

"What year is this, a two thousand?"

"No a ninety-nine."

"A car this old, it's probably the starter. You may need a new one."

He spoke with a slight twang. My guess was that he was from the southwest.

"Are you a mechanic?"

"No." He grinned as if I paid him the highest compliment. "I just know cars."

"Okay, so what do you suggest?"

"Well me giving you a jump may work temporarily. At least we can get you off the bridge. Then you'll need to get it to a shop immediately. I know a good guy over by me who'll give you a good price."

"And where's that?"

"South Philly."

"You don't sound like you're from South Philly." I snickered.

"I'm not." He smiled. "I'm from the great state of Texas."

"I figured as much."

"What does that mean?"

"Your accent obviously." I grinned then pointed. "And your boots. No men from South Philly wear cowboy boots."

"Sure they do." He smiled. "I bought these on South Street just last month."

Relief settled in my bones. He was a good guy and not a dangerous stranger I'd have to gouge in the eyes later. Sometimes in my line of work, it was easy to forget that people were essentially good for the most part and not a whole bunch of degenerates.

"What's your name?" he asked while lifting up the hood of my car.

"Jade."

"Pretty name. I'm Dallas."

I laughed for the obvious reason, "Not much creativity there."

"Don't be so sure. I'm from the Houston area not Dallas."

"Kind of mean for your mom to name you that then."

"My parents met in Dallas at some sort of rally. It's a long, boring story."

"Why don't you tell me about it after we get my car off of this bridge then."

His eyes bulged a bit. I think my forwardness surprised him. Hell, it surprised me too. I was used to men approaching me, but there was something about the way Dallas looked at me that made me want to make the first move. He was different than the overbearing creeps I usually met, and he was a nice looking guy to boot. Someone I didn't mind getting back on the horse with and breaking the Camden mind trance I'd been under.

"I'll tell you anything you want to know, darlin'."

Dallas ended up being one of the nicest men I'd ever met. That's part of the reason why we were doomed from the start. I didn't realize how fucked up in the head I still was until I started dating him.

He opened doors for me, and I would stare at him in bewilderment. He'd call just to say good night, and I'd stare at the incoming call in annoyance. He bought me flowers for my birthday, which was nice, but I guess I'm not a flowers kind of girl. I didn't even have a vase for them, so I stuck them in a bowl of water and left them on the kitchen counter.

After a date he'd come over to my place and would want to *hold me* or *spoon me* since we weren't ready for sex yet, but I felt smothered. I just wanted him to leave, so I could spend the rest of the night watching game highlights.

I think our most significant difference though was that Dallas detested confrontation. If he thought we were about to disagree on something, he pulled back hard. He'd hang up the phone or if we were together, he'd find excuses to leave. Yet I was determined to make it work.

I think I wanted to prove to myself that I wasn't broken. That I wasn't some sort of broken spirit that could only be in unhealthy relationships or have meaningless one-night stands. I needed to prove to myself that I could be *normal*, and more importantly that I didn't want Camden.

JADE

"I'm glad you called me tonight, darlin'."

"Yeah?"

"I hate it when we argue. You know that."

I called Dallas and asked him out to dinner to Solstice for three reasons. One, Ryan had worked me out like a maniac and I was starving. Two, Dallas complained that we had been seeing each other for weeks and he didn't know much more about me than he did when we first met. So I figured taking him to the tapas lounge that the guys owned would be a step in the right direction. Third, it was evident that if I didn't step out of my comfort zone and try letting him "in" that he was going to end things with me.

"Believe it or not I don't like arguing either, Dallas, but you know I'm a work in progress."

I'd told him a little bit about my past with Tyson.

"The two of us are very different, darlin', but that's what makes us interesting. Everything doesn't need to be a battle between us. Just because you don't agree with something I may ask from you doesn't mean that we need to rip each other to shreds about it."

During our argument, Dallas had called me unnecessarily combative, and that's all I could hear him saying now. That he didn't like who I was, and that he wanted me to be someone different. Someone I wasn't ready to be. Someone I didn't even know if I could be. Same negative shit I heard from my father growing up. Same crap I heard from Tyson. Just delivered differently, with a twang and a smile.

"You ready to order?" I asked uncomfortable with the direction that the conversation was going. "The appetizers are really good here, and I'll go ask Celia to use the premium liquor for our drinks."

"Sounds good," he said sounding disappointed with my diversion from the conversation.

We spent the next hour ordering about four different appetizers, sampling bites off of each other's plates, and talking about the washed up quarterback of his beloved Dallas Cowboys when the Kings sauntered in. If I could have managed to duck out of the back door, God knows, I would have.

By that point I had successfully kept Dallas away from my meddling bosses (especially Cam) for weeks, but it was obvious that someone at the restaurant had been persuaded to rat on me. Cutter might have come by once in a while to grab a drink and flirt with Celia, but Camden never ate there. It was no coincidence. They had been tipped off.

It was almost a game between us. Even before the hotel sex with Camden, if I messed around with a guy for too long, they would proceed to scare him away. They claimed it was all for shits and giggles. Harmless fun. But I think those two sadists took a very sick pleasure in spooking off my fuck buddies. If me sleeping with a guy didn't benefit the business, then I suppose they didn't see the point. Freakin' hypocrites.

Lucky for them that I didn't care when they sabotaged me, because by that point I was usually done with the guy anyway, but Dallas was different. I didn't want them scaring him off. He deserved better than to be pitted in the middle of their childish games. Plus I wasn't ready for him to exit my life. I was *trying* with him, especially because I was trying to forget someone else.

"Sharing a romantic dinner I see." Cutter observed while picking up an egg roll off of my plate and popping it in his mouth.

I smacked his hand away.

"You boys are being very rude," I scolded. "As you can see, I'm having dinner with a friend and you weren't invited."

"Dallas, right?" Cutter asked rhetorically.

My stomach dropped. I had no idea that anyone knew that I was seeing Dallas, and if they knew his name then they knew other shit too. This wasn't good.

Camden was standing quietly to the side observing the entire exchange, leaning back against the bar, his thickly corded arms crossed in front of his chest. His eyes were keenly focused on Dallas, but he didn't say a word. He didn't have to. His icy cold eyes said it all.

Dallas startled me a moment with the grating sound the legs of the table made across the floor when he abruptly pushed himself away from it. "Can I help you?" I could hear a bit more of his southwestern twang angrily reveal itself.

"Well the first thing that you can do, country boy, is sit the fuck back down," Cutter responded in an amused voice.

"Is *this* somebody I should actually give a shit about?" Dallas asked me. I was shocked. He wasn't someone who usually liked to face-off with people. At least I didn't think he was. I honestly never thought that he was a punk or anything, but I never imagined he would have stood up to Cutter like that. He definitely wasn't scared of my idiot bosses, or if he was, he did a good job covering it up. Another good reason to keep him around.

I threw my hand up to stop both of them from saying something else before the exchange ventured down a dangerous road. Cutter could be ... unpredictable.

"Wait. Stop," I said to Cutter.

"I didn't do anything but ask a simple question. Your country fried friend here is a little touchy if you ask me."

I sigh in exasperation.

"Cutter, this is my friend Dallas. We've been seeing each other for a while now, and I'd like to continue doing so. You're making a bad first impression. He's going to think that you guys are unfriendly," I said while giving him the side eye.

Cutter turned and looked towards Camden. "Little bit here says that this guy is her friend. I thought we knew all of her friends."

"Guess not," Camden replies with a stoned face.

Cutter points to Dallas's chair. "Sit."

"Cutter, please—"

"I said have a seat, country boy. No need to get all huffy."

Dallas looks at Cutter, then Camden, and then looks at me. Still not sitting.

"Who are *they*, Jade?"

"Well you wanted to know more about me. I guess you should have been more careful what you wished for. These two baskets of sunshine are my employers."

I hadn't talked much about my job with Dallas. It's hard to explain what I do with regular folks. Sometimes I stretch the truth, and say we're private investigators if I'm forced to talk about it at all, but Dallas never pushed the topic.

"You need to think about getting a new job," he said still standing while Cutter worked on my second egg roll.

"We've got a comedian, Cam," Cutter said while licking his fingers.

The temperature of the room dropped ten degrees as

soon as I looked at Camden's face. This was going to be so bad.

"Let's just go, Dallas." I decided while pushing my chair back and standing up.

"Sit the fuck back down, Jade," Camden ordered in a seriously scary voice.

A bent out of shape Dallas slammed his hands on the table. Some of our appetizers went flying in Cutter's lap, and some of them ended up on the floor. People started to stare.

"Stop talking to her like that," he said to Camden through gritted teeth.

Cutter looked to Camden as if he was requesting permission to sucker punch Dallas first. I knew that look. I'd seen it many times.

"Wait—" I tried to intercede.

"I'll talk to her however, wherever and whenever I fucking please," Camden stepped up closer to the table and said in a deadly tone. "You'd do best to remember that shit."

I just wanted to get Dallas out of there, because he was very much outnumbered. Not just by those two, but because Solstice was full of kitchen staff who were ex-convicts. Everybody in the kitchen would have no problem coming out to fight if they thought the Kings needed back up. As if the two of them *ever* needed back up.

"Let's just go, Dallas," I pleaded. "I'm serious. Let's just go."

"He can get the fuck out of my restaurant, but *you* are going to sit back down. You're not leaving with him."

"You're being ridiculous, Cam. What's wrong with you?"

Cutter's body began shaking with silent, obnoxious laughter.

"What are you laughing at?" I practically screamed. Spit flying out of my mouth.

Camden walked over and stood directly behind me bending his head down by my ear and caging me in completely with his long, thick arms and large body. His palms flat on the table.

"Calm down, you're causing a scene," he quietly requested.

I tried escaping his hold, but I couldn't make him budge. I was pretty sure Dallas was about to punch him in the face when Cutter gave him a warning glare.

"In about ten more seconds this isn't going to end well for you, country boy. I highly recommend you leave now. It's not worth it. She's just entertainment for you, but she belongs to us."

They had taken their game entirely too far. I mentally started plotting a thousand ways that I was going to get my revenge. I'd make sure every woman in the club wouldn't come within ten feet of either of their dicks for a long ass time. I just needed to concoct the perfect rumor. Disease? Impotence? Bankruptcy!

"Just leave, Dallas. Let me deal with them, and I'll call you later. I promise," I said while still being smothered by one soon to be dead King brother. "They must want their *mommy's* attention really badly if they've resorted to acting like this."

Dallas was red as a beet as he watched me squirm under Camden.

"I don't care who they are to you. I'm *not* leaving you here with these assholes."

I tried my best to turn around and knee Camden in his balls, but I still couldn't move freely inside of his tight grip. The big fucker.

"He's not who you think he is," Camden said loud enough for everyone to hear but in a very low, deep and thick timbre that rumbled through my entire body. I imagined it was a voice he used right when he was about to cut a guy's balls off although it was eerily similar to the one he used when he was just about to come inside of me.

"I don't want to hear it," I said angrily. It was pretty clear he'd done some digging into Dallas's personal life and found something that I didn't want to hear. I wish he would have just minded his own business for once in his life.

"Let her go," Dallas warned Camden again.

"Pretty please, Cam?" Cutter interrupted with a facetious request to hit Dallas, but it was pretty obvious that it was Camden's show to run.

"Afraid of what I may have to share, *Dallas?*" Camden said his name like it disgusted him.

"Hell, no. Say whatever you have to say." Dallas prodded him on with confidence. "I want to hear it. Who do you think I am?"

"I told you I don't want to hear it," I said again. My ears covered by my hands.

"Sorry, tiny tot." Camden gently pulled my hands away from my ears. "But you need to hear this. Your new friend here filed a joint tax return this year. He's married and has a three-year-old kid."

I immediately looked up at Dallas for any sign that what I had just heard was wrong, but his face revealed the truth. He had been completely exposed. And in that moment I started to really despise Camden.

Didn't he understand I would never survive the two of us being fuck buddies? That it wasn't healthy or normal for either of us really? Now that they had uncovered Dallas's secret, there was no turning back. I couldn't fuck a married man, and even if I could, those assholes would never let it happen.

"We're separating." Dallas quickly offered up a typical married man's excuse.

"You're separating?" I parrot back slowly wanting to believe it but knowing more than likely it was a lie.

"Bullshit," Camden whispered harshly in my ear.

"I should have told you, but I knew it'd be a deal breaker for you. You'd think it would be too messy, but I swear that I haven't been with Mikayla for over two years."

Hearing her actual name said out loud made me cringe. It made it all the more real.

"You filed a joint return," I countered.

"Because we're still married, but we're separated. We live separate lives."

"Did you fill them out married filing separately or married filing jointly?" I asked grasping at straws.

"Jointly," Camden eagerly added.

I remember thinking how I couldn't wait to kick Camden's ass once this was over.

"I guess you haven't been over his house?" Cutter chimed in.

I looked at Cutter's still face. He stopped munching on my dinner, and he wasn't amused anymore. I was so busy trying to stay in control of everything by making sure he came to my house, that I didn't even consider the fact that he never even invited me over once.

"No, I haven't."

How could I have been so stupid to fall for the oldest game in the book?

"You know why I didn't ask you over, Jade."

"Why?" Cutter asks. "We're dying to know."

"Jade—" Dallas says.

I know what he's claiming. That he didn't ask me over because we agreed that sex was off the table for a while, and that when it happened it would be on my terms and probably at my place. But I damn sure didn't want Camden knowing that. He needed to think I was fucking other people.

"Do you live with her?" I ask cutting him off, so that my own secret isn't exposed.

"I don't. I swear. I have my own apartment, but divorce is long and expensive, it's just taking us a while to settle everything."

"Liar," Camden whispered in my ear.

I already knew Dallas was lying. I could hear the desperation in his voice. I just hated that it was ending this way. Badly. In front of an audience.

"And your kid?" I asked.

"A boy," Camden added smugly.

"Wait are those tears welling up, country boy?" Cutter chuckled.

"Things with my son are ... complicated."

"I bet," Camden said in my ear again.

I'd had enough. I needed to end this.

"You should go, Dallas. I do a lot of dumb shit, but I don't fuck married men. Especially ones with babies."

"That a girl!" Cutter cheered.

"Shut up, Cutter, and *you*," I turned my head, "stop talking in my fucking ear!"

I tried wiggling out of my human Camden cage once again.

"Jade, please—" Dallas tried appealing to me one more time.

"No, Dallas. I can't do it. Lose my number and have a nice life."

After a dejected looking Dallas finally walked out of Solstice, Camden finally released me, and I promptly turned around and smacked the hell out of him.

I put my whole body into it and got a good smack in. My palm was burning, and his face was even turning red under that five o'clock shadow of his, yet that asshole didn't even flinch.

"If you think I'm going to sit idly by while you try to fuck me out of your system, then you've sorely misjudged me."

I was speechless by his words and by the venom in which he spewed them.

Then Cutter raised his arm to get the server's attention.

"Garlic wings and a round of drinks over here please. We're celebrating!"

"Celebrating what?" I almost whisper.

"Progress," he answered.

CAMDEN

My great-grandfather owned a small supermarket in the meat district of Philadelphia. It was always his dream to pass the store down to his son and so on and so on. I've heard the story a million times. My grandfather was seventeen years old and working part time in the market when *they* came knocking. It's not an urban myth or fiction that organized crime exists. It does. And it certainly did back in those days.

If you wanted to do business back in those days you had to pay. You had to pay the government, you had to pay the city, you had to pay your landlord and you had to pay the mob. My great-grandfather had a difficult time accepting that cold hard truth and eventually paid the price. He tried organizing several of the businesses in the area to stand up against the mob. It only took three days for retaliation.

Benjamin King's throat was slit right behind the cold cuts counter in front of his son, my grandfather, as a warning to all the other store owners in the area. Not being paid and organizing some sort of rebellion wouldn't be tolerated.

They allowed my grandfather to live to spread the word, and to serve as a living example of their ruthlessness and their mercy.

My grandfather was traumatized by this event needless to say. Back in those days there was no PTSD diagnosis. There wasn't treatment for it. People just called you batshit crazy. And God bless him, but he was definitely batshit crazy.

I'm not really sure how he talked my grandmother into marriage, but I think it had something to do with her desperately wanting to get out of her parents home. Marriage was the only way back in those days for most women. My grandfather wasn't much of a provider. He lost the market, and only seemed to be able to hold onto menial jobs, but my grandmother worked as an elementary school teacher for well over thirty years and was a good provider. She was good to my grandfather, tolerated his lunacy, and gave him two children. One of them being my father.

My father, Benjamin King The Third, was a dickhead. Having a good mother didn't make up for the fact that he was named after and was raised by a father with tons of issues. He resented his own father and lived with a mission to never be like him, which he succeeded in some ways, but failed in others.

At first things were pretty average as far as family dynamics went. Financially he did much better than his own father. He built a small printing business, which afforded us a nice life in a middle class neighborhood with pretty decent schools. But things were changing rapidly in the city where we lived and our father was not prepared for change.

Lots of companies who faithfully used his business were closing. The Internet and growing use of email and digital documents was growing. Due to a decrease in jobs in the city, many families were flocking to the suburbs, and virtually overnight we watched our neighborhood change.

Watching his business slowly unravel and become irrelevant grew to be too much for him. He started drinking heavily and running with a group of men who were small time hustlers to make ends meet.

Cutter and I were eleven and twelve years old when he started taking us out on runs. He always wanted us to have the car running and waiting in case he had to leave somewhere quickly. Sometimes he would stop at massage parlors for a payoff pick up and would bring us inside. He'd pay a new girl to give us both hand jobs while he got the full service package in another room.

There was an abandoned field near our neighborhood that was starting to be used as a makeshift firing range. It was fucking dangerous but he took us there anyway and taught us both how to shoot. It's why we're both good shots to this day. Our training was inappropriate and much of it was self-serving, but our father did leave us with a couple of life lessons before he was a victim of a deal gone bad.

It was a run like so many others but karma had come to bite him in the ass. Someone had held a gun to his head and stuck him up months back, and he never went back to deal with him. Probably because he was too drunk to remember who the thief was. That same guy came back to rob him a second time and killed our father. A shot right to the head.

We were both waiting in the car.

Our father's death served as the foundation upon which me and my brother's ultra tight relationship was formed. At only a year apart, I was never really his older brother. We were always a team. Working together to take our father's place as the head of the house. Helping our mother in any way we could. We had to step up and become the men of the house and make money the best way we knew how. With our smarts and our fists. We had each other's back and we always will. There's nothing I wouldn't do for Cutter, and I know the sentiment is mutual.

~

"What do you think you're doing?"

I walk into the carriage house that my brother and I share and catch him using one of my laptops. I usually carry my main one everywhere with me in my leather backpack, but I have a couple others that I store at home. I use them almost like burner phones. Work on them a few times then toss them. I make sure to assign a VPN proxy server to all of my machines, so that I can use various anonymous IP addresses. This enables me to track and hack without leaving a trail for the average techie to trace.

"Just checking on something." He closes all of the browser windows he had open and closes the laptop.

"On one of my burner machines? Why aren't you on your own computer? This better not be about the glamazon."

Cutter and I are as close as two brothers can be. We share everything. But sometimes we both can hold back on information when we're not ready to share it with the other. I've known for a while that he's been sabotaging Elizabeth's friend Sloan aka the glamazon. She's the daughter of a famous NBA player and she's a party girl. From my observation, she's got lots of beauty but not much substance. Cutter's watched me long enough to know how to do a basic tap on a phone or a hack into an email server. So he knows how to snoop. At first I thought it was funny. Harmless play. But now I'm wondering.

"And what if it is?"

"You're using company resources to sabotage a woman's life."

"Sabotage is a strong word, brother, and I am a partner in this company too."

"Toy with then. Is that a better word?"

"I just want to see who she's talking to."

"Why? I'm honestly confused as to why you would want anything to do with that spoiled brat?"

"Watch your mouth."

"What did you fucking say?" I ask in disbelief that he's defending her.

"I haven't made any judgment calls about whatever the fuck you're doing with the little lima bean now have I?"

"I don't know what I'm doing," I confess.

"I know you don't, but you're doing *something*, and I've been backing you a hundred percent of the way. Didn't I call you when she got pissy drunk with Marco? Weren't you the first one I told that Patrick came sniffing around for her? Wasn't my intel on that Dallas prick correct?"

"Cut—"

"You worry too much, big brother. I'm on a simple fishing expedition. Nothing more."

He was right. I was projecting my own shit onto him. It wasn't fair. I was the one toying with someone's life. Keeping her stuck inside of the club. Knowing that she'd probably hate me for it.

"How many times have you used this laptop?"

"Just today."

"You can use it about two more times. Then toss it."

"Understood."

"So tell me. You haven't said a word about it yet."

"Tell you what?"

"What do you think about Jade?"

"What I've always thought."

"Little sister?"

"Not exactly."

"What do you mean?"

"I'd be lying if I said I never gave her a second glance."

My brow furrows. "Meaning?"

"Meaning she is a beautiful woman. That's all I'm saying. A man would have to be dead not to notice her."

"And the fact that she's like family?"

"Complicated but not insurmountable."

I feel better now that we've actually cleared the air. I would never admit to it, but I feel much better that I have his approval. Although I think I need to make something clear from the get go.

"She's not like the others, Cutter."

"Obviously." He grins.

"I mean I don't think she would be up for sharing."

Cutter and I have often shared women. Not all the time, but a majority of the time. It started in high school almost as a necessity. After our father's death, our mom turned the smaller third bedroom in our house into a workroom. She was a wedding dress seamstress on the side.

So Cutter and I resorted to sneaking girls into the bedroom that we shared, and it wasn't like one of us was going to pretend we were asleep. That's just not in our natures. So sometimes we would watch. Sometimes when the girl was willing we would participate. A lot of the times that meant one of us was keeping their mouths busy with our tongues or our dicks, so that the sounds of orgasms wouldn't wake our mother. It grew to be something that we were skilled at and that we enjoyed. I never thought about us *not* sharing a woman until Jade.

"That's what we've mistakenly thought about a lot of women over the years. She might surprise you."

"Not this time."

"Are you saying that *you* don't want to share her?"

Is that what I'm saying?

"I'm saying that I barely got her into bed once. The thought of you jumping in is sure to send her running for the hills."

"How about we just play it by ear, Cam. Remember that Jade belonged to all of *us* way before she just belonged to you."

JADE

The heavy rain outside is causing a constant thrumming sound against the walls of Lotus. I love the sound of a storm. All the crashing sounds of the wind and thunder make me think of sex. Powerful sex. Which puts me completely on edge, because King Kong is staring right at me. All settled into his perch up high. A scotch on one side of him. His laptop on another.

I'm sitting at the bar next to the previous night's receipts, when a soaking wet distraction, dressed in all violet, comes running through the door. So I pull my eyes away from his sexy highness to see what *it* wants.

"You're Jade right?"

"Who's asking?"

"My name is Mirna."

"And …"

"And I'd like to arrange a meeting with your employers. I heard you were the woman to speak to."

"Is that right."

"Was that incorrect information?"

"No."

"Uh, okay, so …"

"What do you need to speak to them specifically about?"

"I'd like to hire them."

"For what?"

"Well that would be between me and them. The job is confidential."

"Not if you want me to arrange it."

"Can you just tell him that I'm Joe K's friend. He'll know who that is."

"He? I thought you said you wanted to hire *them*."

"Well I'd really like to speak specifically to one of them. He was recommended for my particular job."

"You want Roman?"

"No, not him. I want Camden. Camden King."

She starts darting her eyes around the club. Fortunately the lights are slightly dimmed upstairs, so she can't see Camden watching and no doubt listening to us from the second level.

"Camden, huh? Umm, I don't think so."

"Sheesh, I didn't know it was going to be so difficult to make a simple appointment. I didn't know he had a wife or warden or whatever you are."

"Be assured that I'm ALL of that."

"Did anyone ever tell you that you're a bit of a bitch?"

I hear Camden's booming laughter over the white noise of movement in the club. Normally I'd throw him the bird, but not while Miss Mirna's standing here.

"Not the right attitude if you want any help from me, ma'am," I say.

"Ma'am!?"

"Just trying to be respectful. The lines around your mouth tell me that you've probably got to be a good ten years older than me, and my mother taught me manners. Respect my elders and all that good shit."

"You're fucking kidding right?"

"No, ma'am."

"I don't have to deal with this attitude. Just … give him my information."

"Yeah, ma'am, I'll get right on that."

After old Miss Mirna leaves the club in a huff, I'm immediately summoned like I knew I would be.

"Jade, get your ass up here in my office. Now."

"I'm here. What is it?" I ask as if I don't already know that he's about to rip me a new asshole for tossing potential money out the door.

"Lock the door."

"I don't think that's a good idea."

"What?"

"In case I gotta run," I try joking.

"Lock the damn door."

I'm stuck in place, leaning face first against the door, after locking it. A small feeling is gnawing at my gut to open it back up and *run*, but I've never run from a fight in my life, and I'm not going to start now.

Bass heavy dance music begins pulsing below us. The deejay must be starting his warm up, because I can literally feel the buzz of the speakers coming straight through the floor. The song isn't familiar to me, but I like it, and the hypnotic beat seems to be synchronizing with the cadence of my heart.

"That woman was a paying client," Camden argues.

I don't dare turn around, but I can hear and feel him coming near me.

"You don't know that."

"She asked for me specifically."

"You don't know that it was really about business."

He presses his heavily scented body against mine in all its earthy goodness.

I close my eyes and pray for a hail Mary.

"You were cock blocking," he says while sliding one of his massive hands under the back of my shirt. Then around my waist. Then down the front of my leggings. "I think I'm starting to appreciate these pants of yours now. Easy access."

I don't respond. I can't. I think if I say anything, he would stop, and it feels too good for him to stop. He hasn't touched me in so long. Heaven help me, but I miss his touch.

"I promised myself I wouldn't touch you again until you asked me to, Jade, but I think I seriously underestimated how stubborn you are."

I gasp when he buries his other hand into my hair, and pulls my head back while simultaneously sliding the opposite hand farther between my slippery folds. His words making me slicker and slicker.

"I've put a lot of thought into when I'd take you again. It was going to be some romantic shit, because you probably haven't had a lot of that in your life. We'd dress up. There'd be flowers. Wine. And maybe a nice hotel room at the end of the night for nostalgia's sake."

He pulls his hand out of my pants and into his own. I can hear him unbuckling his belt and pulling the heavy leather strap he always wears slowly through the belt loops of his jeans.

"But now I'm realizing that even though that's what I think you deserve, it doesn't mean that's what you really need, and I've made it my sole mission to give you what you need. At least for the next thirty days."

The volume of the music downstairs is growing louder. I can feel it swirling through my body. I'm flushed, I'm anxious, I'm excited, and I'm petrified.

"Cam—"

"Shhh," he says by my ear. "You're killing us both, Jade. Let me put us both out of our misery."

He uses the same hand in my hair to move me away from the door and bend me over the desk.

"Move whatever you need out of your way," he orders.

"Your laptop," I breathlessly mention out of concern.

"I don't fucking care, Jade," he growls. "If you want it out of the way, if you want me, then move it."

For once I get out of my head and just act. Sliding everything on the desk onto the floor in a thunderous crash. Amazed that this man wants me so badly, that he doesn't care what gets destroyed in the process.

He yanks my leggings down to my ankles.

"Step out and stay there."

He walks around to the other side of the desk slowly. Each booted step making a heavy thud. Pulling off his thermal shirt he exposes his tat covered abs and chest. His pants are open. His dick brick hard, dying to burst through. The hunger in his eyes mirrors the yearning in mine. He looks at me and the destruction I've made of his desk with almost a master's approval.

"Give me your hands."

He takes the belt and binds my hands together then ties the belt to the metal handle of the large desk drawer. The one that's always locked. The desk is wide enough that my small body is fully stretched in an immovable ninety-degree angle across it.

"You look beautiful in this position. Perfect. As we build the trust between us, I won't have to tie your hands up like this, you'll hold them still for me without me having to ask. But since we both know how you like to fight, I thought it would be best if we start like this."

My eyes are blinking faster than normal, because honestly I'm speechless. I've heard rumors about how *creative*

Camden was in bed, and he is, but this is different. He didn't treat me like this in Baltimore. He was assertive, but he wasn't domineering. He was holding back, and now I'm afraid I've unleashed something or someone that I'm in no way ready to handle.

"I know this might be difficult for you. You're used to calling the shots and running circles around those losers you usually fuck. I even allowed you to dictate a lot of what went down between us in Baltimore, but I promise you, Jade, that what you're going to learn is that surrendering control to me is going to be the most freeing thing you've ever felt in your life."

He rubs his palm up and down my back in a massaging motion. Soothing my frayed nerves. I'm on edge like I've never been before in my life, because I don't know what to expect, and I don't know how to control it, but I think I'm excited by it.

Smack!

What the hell? He slaps my butt with the same hand that was just so tender with me ten seconds ago.

"Oww!" I gripe.

"Don't ever turn money away again. I don't care if that woman said she wanted to suck my dick. If she wanted to hire me, then she was a potential client. Money is money."

"Fuck that—"

Smack!

The second time Camden slaps me, it stings as well, but something's different. The sound of his hand against my ass, his gruff voice, the position I'm in, the thrill of knowing that someone could actually see me in this position if they knocked on that door has a tingling sensation radiating through my ass that feels exquisite. So good that I let out a small moan that I wish I could take back.

"You like that don't you."

Smack!

"I knew you would."

Then he slides his hand between my legs.

"You're gushing wet, Jade, and you owe me money."

I can hear the crinkling of what I am pretty sure is a condom packet being ripped open behind me.

"How are you going to work it off?" he teases.

Before I can come up with a snarky answer, like he can take his money and shove it up his ass, his pants are down and he enters me swiftly and deeply.

"Fuck," I groan.

Smack!

He hits my ass again. "Spread your legs. I'm going deeper."

I'm holding on for dear life to the belt strap tethering my body to the desk as he rocks my body forward and back with deep, heavy thrusts. My breasts threatening to burst through my bullshit ten-dollar bra as they rub against the desk. I'm loving everything that he's doing. The way he's taking me assertively, but not too roughly. How full I feel by his girth. How his desire for me seems to grow with each commanding stroke.

"Wider," he demands.

"Dammit," I cry and quiver as his cock travels farther inside of me inch-by-inch.

"Who do you belong to, Jade?" he grunts.

I'm not going to say it. I refuse to say his name. A girl has to have some sort of dignity. At least I take some satisfaction in knowing that he's enjoying this just as much as I am.

Smack!

I bury my face into the crook of my arm in an effort to muffle the scream caused by the cataclysmic orgasm that contracts every muscle in my body. Little bursts of light flicker inside of my head, making me feel lightheaded, as I feel Camden's dick throbbing inside of me. Finding a release of his own.

My body feels like a wet noodle.

Relaxed and slippery.

I'm drenched in sweat and my own juices.

I'm coming down off of my orgasm when I hear Camden bending down behind me. I'm too tired to fight what's coming next.

His hands grab my thighs and pulls them gently apart again. He buries his head in between my legs. His tongue lightly lapping at my sensitive bud. Another orgasm slowly begins to wind inside of me but slows its ascent as soon as Camden stops to *talk* of all things!

"I'm going to Miami this week."

"Okay," I say quickly. Wanting him to get back to what he was doing.

He chuckles. "I want you to behave while I'm gone."

He begins massaging my clit with his thumb.

"Okay," I concede. "I'll behave."

"That's good to hear. And Jade?"

"Yes?" I moan.

Just feeling his breath so close to my pussy as he talks is making me grow wetter.

"Whether you say it or not, your pussy belongs to me. I think I've proven that tonight."

Before I can respond, his mouth descends onto my engorged clit and he takes a strong pull. And in less than ten seconds flat, I'm pulling for dear life on that fucking belt.

JADE

Since Camden and Roman are in Miami for a week, I have decided to take full advantage of the fact that I am the acting manager of Lotus, and delegate my ass off. Cutter's busy all week with the baseball player that the guys handle, so it's totally my show.

On Monday night I give Marco the honors of opening and closing. Mondays are half-price on whatever's on tap. We get a lot of newbies on Monday nights. People who normally wouldn't get in on the busy nights. We use the house deejay and only need minimal staff working, so I feel pretty confident that Marco can handle it.

I spend the entire day pampering myself. I get my hair blown out. A manicure and pedicure. Pink gel on the hands and a darker shade of hot pink on my toes. And during my ninety-minute hot stone massage, I get a call that I can't ignore.

"Hello?" I answer in a dreamy like state.

"What the *fuck* are you doing? Why do you sound like that?"

Of course it can only be Camden.

"Hey, *King Kong*," I say in a sultry voice. Motioning to the masseuse to continue with what feels like God's work.

"That mouth."

"Mmmm."

"Do you want me to come home, Jade? Is that why you're testing me like this?"

"I'm getting a massage which you're interrupting by the way."

"You should be at the club."

"It's too early to sit in that dark ass club. Why are you trying to regulate my life from all the way there?"

I look at the clock on the wall.

"Wait, you can't even be in Miami yet. Where are you calling me from?"

"The plane."

Now I notice it. The tension in his voice.

"Do you not like flying, King Kong?"

I give the masseuse the one moment signal and sit up on the table.

"Not really."

"Shouldn't the plane have taken off already?"

"Yeah but we haven't taxied yet. Something about waiting our turn in line. They're letting us use our phones in the meantime. I didn't know you liked massages."

"I haven't had one in a long time."

"Where are you getting it?"

"A place in Olde City."

"Expensive."

"My boss pays me the big bucks so I splurged," I kid. "Why don't you like to fly?"

"Turbulence."

"Big badass Camden King is afraid of a little turbulence? The man I know isn't afraid of anything."

"That's where you're wrong. Flying in the air isn't natural,

Jade. I'm not ashamed of a little healthy fear. That's how I know I'm alive."

"It's safer then driving a car."

"I'm sure you read that misleading statistic somewhere and just automatically believed it."

"I think you're the one that needs to believe it. You're the one who's going to be up in the air really soon."

"Thanks a lot."

"You're welcome." I giggle. "Listen, nothing's going to happen all right? You're on a short flight. You're on a reputable airline. I bet the captain is well rested and knows how to handle himself when a little choppiness starts."

"You're right."

"I know I'm right. Plus, if something ever happened to you think of all the trouble I would get myself into."

"Fucking true."

His voice sounds better.

"Look, my therapist is giving me the stink eye."

"All right."

"Call me when you land," I demand.

He pauses for a moment.

"I will, baby."

I pay my masseuse double to go over the original time and reschedule her next appointment with a different therapist. Now I am starting to understand why the boys are so quick to throw their money at situations and at people. It works.

I am feeling absolutely blissful after my massage ends and now I think I should top the entire day off with a good meal. There's a local Italian spot close to my apartment building that would be a perfect place for a little linguine and clams. After ordering my meal and a glass of white wine, I get a call from my sister of all people.

"Twice in the same year?" I say when I answer her call.

"Funny, Jade. What are you doing?"

"Having dinner."

"Ooh, with the twin?"

"No, Jana. How can I help you tonight?"

"I was taking a break from writing a paper and thought about you."

"Were you writing about sibling rivalry?"

"Ha, ha. No. I was writing a paper on the psychological effects of family members caring for a relative with Alzheimer's—"

"And what pray tell does that have to do with me?"

"Well, Alzheimer's makes me think of older people. Sick people. Which in turn made me think of Dad and how you won't talk to him. And there you have it. That's how I thought of you."

"You need to conduct a study on yourself. You know what they say about the definition of insanity. Doing the same thing over and over and expecting different results. I've told you a thousand times, I'm not talking to our sperm donor."

I take a bite of my bread dipped in olive oil.

"What are you eating?"

"Linguine and clams."

"Mom's favorite?"

"One of her favorite's, yes."

"Tell me a story about Mom."

"I'm not a good story teller, Jana, and frankly I'm not in the mood to talk about Mom."

"Tell me anyway. You remember her so much better than I do."

I take a sip of my wine.

"She was a singer. A sing in the shower type singer. She

didn't sing in a choir or anything like that. But there was this one time, when I signed up for the third grade talent show."

"You did?"

"I had no idea what I was doing when I signed up. There was a sheet going around and all the kids were signing up, so I did too. When Mrs. Patasky asked me what song I had selected for my solo, I almost vomited my soft pretzel from lunch right there on her desk."

"Ugh, I couldn't stand Mrs. Patasky. She was a horrible teacher."

"So anyway, I was so horrified that I got myself into this ridiculous situation, I didn't tell Mom. I just told her I was part of the talent show and what night to show up."

"Did Dad come?"

"No, Jana. He never came to shit. How can you not remember that?"

"Sorry, sorry, go ahead."

"So Mom came, and you were there too in pigtails and a red checkered dress."

"I've seen that dress in pictures. I remember."

"So we weren't allowed to sing anything suggestive in the show which basically cut out everything they were playing on the radio back then, so I had to go with a Disney hit. Aladdin's 'A Whole New World.'"

"Sheesh, you had to sing one of the hardest ones."

"When I got up there, I didn't just feel nerves, I felt like there was a war raging inside of my chest."

"What did you do?"

"I looked at Mrs. Patasky with pitiful eyes, but she wasn't taking the bait. The talent show was her baby and she didn't want to look like a complete failure in front of the entire school, so she gave me that infamous Patasky glare and cued the music."

"Why that woman didn't have you all rehearse the show is unfathomable to me. So then what happened?"

I take another sip of my wine. My mouth dry from talking.

"I opened my mouth and barely a peep came out. It was like my vocal chords were saying *oh hell no, bitch, not today*. I remember how the audience was staring at me. Waiting with bated breath for me to sing a note."

"And then?"

"And then I saw Mom excusing herself with you in tow down the aisle. Then up the steps and onto the stage. She asked them to kindly cue the music again, because the Barlow girls were going to do a group number."

"What! I don't remember that."

"Of course you don't, you were a baby."

"I was in kindergarten I think."

"Exactly, a baby. Anyway Mom grabbed my hand and stepped us both to the mic, and when she started singing, gosh, you could hear a pin drop in the auditorium. She was amazing. She hit every note."

"What did I do?"

"You were twittering around the stage like the nut job you are. You believed yourself to be a serious dancer at the time. Not singers like us."

"And then what happened?"

"Then we received a standing ovation and some of the kids at lunch gave me their good snacks for three days straight. I was popular for like a week, and I had the most talked about performance that year."

"Wow, Mom was so cool."

"She was."

"So, Jade …"

"Yeah?"

"About Daddy."

"I'm hanging up, Jana."

"Wait ... I'm not just asking for him. I'm asking for you. Imagine how much better *you'll* feel if you forgive him."

"I'll *feel* like yanking the IV out of his arm to speed things along."

"Sheesh, you're a beast. You'll never change."

"Exactly, Dr. Barlow, now go write a paper on that shit."

An hour and another glass of wine later.

Cutter: Where the hell are you?

Crap.

Me: What do you mean?

Cutter: Don't try that sweet bullshit with me. I'm not Cam.

Me: You miss me, King Cutter?

He likes that nickname.

Cutter: Stop with the bullshit and get your tiny ass in here and do your job.

Me: All right already! I have to go home and change real quick. I'll be there in thirty.

Cutter: Make it twenty

That King brother has way too much time on his hands. Unless Camden has requested that his brother keep tabs on me. Yeah, maybe that's it. I wouldn't put it past him.

After running home for a quick shower and to change into a black sleeveless top, dark jeans, my boots and a black puffer coat, I notice that my unwanted guest is not sitting inside of his blue Honda. Interesting. It would be a great time to do a little snooping.

I try each door and stumble upon a backseat door that's open. I reach around and unlock the driver's door, look around my surroundings and hop in. I need to make this quick.

I rummage through the glove compartment, the sun visors, the console between the two front seats, but I don't find much. Just documentation for the car, which matches the name and address on his license. Insurance. Vehicle registration. AAA membership. I also notice an old speeding ticket, but after a closer glance, realize that he isn't the recipient of the ticket. He was the issuer.

Chase is a cop.

Fuck.

I hop out of the car, making sure to put everything back where I found it, get in my rickety death trap and make my way quickly towards the club. I decide to turn the radio off, so I can drive in complete silence. Sometimes the hum of a car engine helps me process, and I certainly have some thinking to do.

Cutter greets me at the door. "Thank you for making an appearance at your own club, Manager Barlow."

I look around and turn my lips up. "It's dead in here. You didn't need me."

"It doesn't matter if it's dead in here. You have employees that you're responsible for. But no … you're too busy getting manis and pedis to bother checking in with your place of employment."

"You ARE following me!"

"Nah, you must have told Joan where you were going."

"You better not have a tracker on my cell phone. I will kick your ass and Camden's."

"Calm down, we're not running some sort of secret government surveillance program in here. There's no tracker on your phone."

I don't care what he says. I pull my phone out of my pocket and turn it on. Swiping the screens to check for the appearance of any new apps that I may not have noticed.

"By the way, there's a customer over there asking for you. New guy. Said you told him about the club and a promise of a free drink."

"What? I didn't—"

I look over to where Cutter is pointing and can't fucking believe it. Chase is in Lotus and he looks totally different. He's ditched the hoodie, evidently taken a shower, and looks quite presentable. He nods his head hello, and I respond with a half-hearted smile in response.

"You know this guy?" Cutter suspiciously questions me after noticing my reaction.

"Umm, yeah. I told him about half-price Monday nights. Let me go say hello."

Cutter grabs my forearm to stop me.

"Who is he?"

"Just a guy."

"A guy you met where?"

"In my building."

"New tenant?"

"Cutter, you sound just as bad as your brother."

"The two of us are interchangeable, Jade," he says, giving me a weird look that would almost resemble *heat* if I didn't know better.

"I'm going to go speak to him now."

"Uh, huh. Go ahead."

Great, now Cutter is going to watch me with an eagle eye. I've got to play this just right.

"It's nice to see you stop by." I pat Chase's shoulder as if he's an old friend.

"Thanks, Jade. I heard about half-priced beer and couldn't resist."

He smiles, but it never quite reaches his eyes.

"You mean *I* told you about it," I correct him with a forced grin.

He looks around me and sees Cutter watching us.

"That's what I meant." He smirks. Probably thinking he now has something on me. "I remembered you telling me about it, and so I figured I'd stop by."

"Sure let me get one for you." I wrap my knuckles on the bar. "Hey, Joan, can you get my friend Officer Whitman here, whatever's on tap."

"Sure thing."

Chase looks at me.

I stare at him.

Checkmate.

"You've been doing some investigating I see," he says.

"You seem to know so much about me, I was curious, and I'm pretty sure you just stopping unwanted by my place of employment to harass me constitutes another example of you violating the stalking laws in this state."

"Am I harassing you?"

"Your mere existence is harassment. No more playing games, officer. What do you want?"

"I want a beer and to listen to a little music."

"Outside of my house was one thing, but you coming here is another. You're asking for trouble you don't want. Just because you're a cop means nothing. We know cops too."

"We?"

"Yes, the people that own this place."

"Well I'm off duty tonight. Just a citizen. I want a couple of beers and maybe to dance with a few pretty ladies and that's it. No trouble."

"I want you out."

"Then put me out."

The way he practically spits the words of his last sentence rattle me. It reminds of the one thing that he and Tyson just may have in common. A temper and a very distinct disdain for women. I can tell that he is dying for me to force his hand. I know an itchy finger when I see it. I lived with a man who had one. He wants to hurt me; he's just looking for an excuse.

"Excuse me for a moment and enjoy your drink. It's on the house," I say, then walk away.

He silently nods his head in acceptance of my offer and turns his stool around. I'm pretty sure Joan overheard some of our conversation, because she gives me a quizzical look. I smile to assure her that everything is fine, although I'm not sure she totally bought it.

I speed walk my way upstairs, into the office, and lock the door. I pull out one of Camden's spare laptops to do a deep search on one *Officer Chase Whitman. Annapolis, Maryland.* Camden uses some sort of special search engine on his computers that the average person doesn't know about.

My mouth is agape after my search. Chase is definitely a cop. A crooked cop. After a two-year investigation, and a suspension without pay, Chase was released from duty. Separate and apart from that case, and before he was suspended, Chase was also the lead investigator on an Annapolis cold case involving one twenty-three-year-old victim named, Tyson Whitman.

Tyson was exactly twenty-three years old when we split up. Was he murdered back then? Could Chase think that I actually have something to do with his death? Now it makes sense. How could I have been so stupid. He was totally behind the chain of emails that drew me to Baltimore. Everything seemed so legit. I even tracked the IP address of the damn things. I actually thought I was meeting a distant relative of my mother's. Someone who could share more memories of her with me. Someone, if it panned out, would be family for me and Jana to connect with. Unfortunately, my desperation for a connection has led a possible sociopath to my door. I close the laptop, and consider what I need to do. How I need to handle this.

Someone begins turning on the knob of the office and shaking the door to try and open it. I start to panic a little. Chase being inside of Lotus, knowing where I live, and discovering what his true source of motivation may be has got me rattled.

"Who is it?"

"It's me. Open the door."

I run to the door and let Cutter in hoping the fear in my voice doesn't register. Cutter stands directly in front of me, quietly assessing my face, in an effort to determine for himself what's going on with me.

"Something's wrong."

I bend my head down to hide from him.

"Something ... is wrong," I admit.

"Is it the guy downstairs?"

I exhale. "Yes."

Cutter proceeds to unlock one of the lock boxes hidden behind the love seat. He pulls out a large, silver gun, checks it for ammo, and then slides it behind his back in his waist.

"Cutter."

"What, munchkin?"

"I haven't even told you who he is."

"It doesn't matter. You're shaking like a leaf."

"I need to ask you something before you go down there."

"What?"

"Do you know what Roman and Camden did to my ex, Tyson?"

"What are you asking about that shithead for?"

"Because the shithead's brother is downstairs, and he's a cop, and I think he thinks we have something to do with Tyson being dead."

Cutter cradles my head between his two enormous hands and looks into my eyes with sincerity.

"I wasn't there, but I can promise you that they didn't have anything to do with that. Camden would have told me."

I jump when the door to the office is kicked open wide.

"Problem is I don't believe that shit," the intruder says snarling.

Chase enters the room and grabs me by the throat with his arm. He quickly closes the door with the bottom of his foot. My neck stuck in the crook of his elbow. A gun pointed at my temple. I can't move.

Cutter steps back and simultaneously pulls out his weapon.

Pointing it at Chase.

His left eye twitching.

His stance relaxed but ready.

"Let her go, and I'll let you walk out of here."

"So you're a cop killer too?"

"I'm not anything but a man that wants you to let go of his friend."

"What is it about this trick anyway?" He squeezes my throat a little harder. "I've been watching her for weeks, seen her naked as a jaybird, and I don't get it. Why are you assholes willing to kill for her?"

Cutter's eye twitches a little more.

"No one in here killed your brother."

"No one in this room? So you're saying it was your

brother that did it? Or perhaps that Roman asshole? Yeah, I think he's the one responsible."

"We can talk about this all night once you let go of Jade."

He squeezes my throat a little tighter. I plead with my eyes for Cutter to stop bringing up my name. Chase doesn't like it, and the angrier he gets, the more I can't breathe.

"It's hard to get that one to make an appearance. I lured Jade to Baltimore in the hopes that he'd follow her. I just assumed she was fucking him and he'd come running. But he didn't come. Only your brother did. Then I started watching her at her apartment. Thinking she'd run to him like usual to tell and that he'd show up there. But this one's a tricky little trick. Seems like she didn't say anything to any of y'all about me."

He tightens his grip yet again.

I can see Cutter is getting agitated.

This negotiation isn't going the way he intended.

"You've got the wrong people," he says through clenched teeth.

"Well this is the thing," Chase says. "I can't just take your word for it. I'm pretty sure the last people who saw my brother alive all work at this shit club. I want us all to have a conversation. On record. And I'll leave your girlfriend alone. You've got forty-eight hours."

"They're not in town."

"Well I guess they better get back in town, or I'll have the feds crawling all over this fixer business bullshit of yours. I'm sure you have a lot of other bodies buried that you don't want turning up."

I feel woozy.

I underestimated this psycho.

He hasn't let up his chokehold on me since he grabbed me.

And I'm starting to lose consciousness.

I think about all sorts of things before I hit the office floor. First, I pray that nothing happens to Cutter. Second, I hope that the screen on my phone doesn't shatter. It's brand new. And third, I hope that Camden had a safe flight.

I miss him.

JADE

I wake up in unfamiliar surroundings. Definitely not the club. I'm in a large bedroom with exposed brick on the walls and wooden beams running across the ceiling. I'm lying in the largest cherry wood four-poster bed I've ever seen and with the softest tan and rust sheets that smell like sandalwood. Smells like … Camden.

My head is pounding. Harder than any hangover I've ever had. And I start to remember. Chase at the club. Him holding me by my neck. A gun at my temple. Cutter with a gun pointed at him trying to save me. I'm alive, but where's Cutter? I try rolling onto my side and feeling around for my phone when I notice a large body asleep in a chair in the corner. Arms folded. Head leaning on the wall behind him. It's Cutter. Thank God.

"Cutter," I try calling out to him with a scratchy throat. "Cutter."

His eyes pop open. "You're awake!"

I try shaking my head yes. It hurts too much to speak, but I'm not really sure why.

"Shhh," he warns me. "Everything probably hurts. You

took a nasty fall when you passed out. I'm sorry about that. I didn't have time to catch you and deal with officer crazy."

"Chase—"

"He's not dead. He was about to be though. Once you fell to the ground, I got the jump on him. My gun was deep in the fucker's mouth, but then Joan came in. Screaming. Asked me if I wanted her to call the police. So what I could I say? No?

Needless to say, he's in a holding cell, and there are some cops itching to get a statement from you once you're up for it. Evidently the guy's been going nuts trying to prove the murder of his brother, so he could earn some brownie points and get his job back. As if anyone gives a shit about the murder of his drug addicted half brother. I think he was grasping at straws with that one if you ask me."

"Where am I?"

"Let me go get you some pain medicine and some water. Maybe a little something to eat. You're in mine and Camden's house. This is Cam's room. He'll be here soon. When the two of those meatheads heard what happened to you, they were on the first thing smoking out of Miami. No one fucks with our girl. Don't you worry, heads will roll on this one. That fucker will never get out of jail. Cam will figure out how to pin about ten different crimes on his ass."

I laugh a little, but it hurts.

"I'll be right back. I know I'm naturally funny, but you've got to stop laughing at the king, all right? You're going to hurt yourself." He smiles.

I shake my head in agreement.

After I take two hospital-strength Motrin that Cutter got from God knows where, I eat a small bowl of chicken and wild rice soup he made for me, and then I lay back down.

"I know you like massages, so I'm going to rub your feet for you. Put your ass right to sleep."

I don't really like random people touching my feet, but I'm too tired to protest, and he's not lying. He gives the best foot rubs ever.

～

Someone is spooning me.

Someone warm and hard.

There's a large, muscular arm tossed across my middle covered in a sleeve full of familiar looking tats.

"I'm home," Camden rumbles by my ear.

"Hi," I manage to eek out.

"How's your head feel?"

"Much better."

"I heard Cutter gave you one of his famous foot massages."

"He did."

"You feel up to a shower?"

"I don't have any clothes here."

"Actually, you do. We took the liberty of bringing over a couple of your things here while you recover. It's not safe at your place. It took me all of five minutes to get in and out of your building with your shit."

"You have my key, jackoff."

"You remembered that?"

"I wasn't that drunk. You slid it right in your back pocket."

"It's amazing to me how selective you are about your drunkenness. Too drunk to willingly consent to me being inside of you in Baltimore. Sober enough at your place to notice that I took your key and then you throw up. Interesting."

"My place is fine. I'll be fine to recover at home."

"Did you know that Chase had been in your apartment?"

Oh my God.

"What?!"

"Exactly. You rethinking your living situation now?"

"Isn't he locked up?"

"Okay, maybe I didn't communicate the right way about this. You're staying here with me for a few days. End of story. No discussion. It's not forever. Just a while. I don't care whether they lock his ass under the jail. It has nothing to do with whether you're staying here or not."

"All I did was fall and bump my head. I'll be fine."

"Correction—you were strangled with a chokehold by a trained police officer until you passed out, fell, and bumped your head."

"Well when you put it like that—"

"When I put it like that, it scares the fuck out of me. When I put it like that, I'm glad that my brother was there. When I put it like that, it makes me consider the fact that I should have listened to my gut and not gotten on that plane. Look what happens when I don't listen."

"Pfft. Don't kid yourself. You wanted to stay home, because you hate to fly." I chuckle as I slowly sit myself up. "It had nothing to do with me."

"Get in the shower and shut up. It'll make you feel a hundred times better."

Camden didn't lie. His shower feels incredible. That's one thing about living in an apartment building, there isn't much you can do about the dismal water pressure. You get what you get, and you don't get upset. But by the time I get out of Camden's shower, I feel like a new person.

I put on a throwback BubbleYum Bubblegum T-shirt and a pair of pink LuLaRoe leggings that were in my carry all bag that Camden packed. I never wear these items out. They are strictly for lounging around my apartment. I thought it was amusing how one of the outfits he selected for me happened to be all pink. I think the secret about what my favorite color is may be exposed.

It's Tuesday night and another slow night at the club, so I don't really need to be there, as if the King brothers were ever going to let me out of their sight again anyway. So I figure I'll watch movies all night. The guys have a killer set up with a theater sized television screen, surround system, and stadium seating in their movie room.

When I come out of the room, I almost choke on my saliva. Camden is wearing nothing but a pair of baggy blue basketball shorts that showcases his mouth watering body and Cutter is wearing a pair of soft red sweats that seem to hug his every nook and cranny. They are beautiful men. Especially Cam. They smile when they notice me.

"Feel better?" Cam asks.

"I do, yes."

"Ready for a movie?" Cutter asks. "I popped popcorn."

"Oh? Neither of you is going to go to the club?"

"Not tonight. Roman's going to check in with Marco. He's got it handled."

"Oh okay, then yeah, I'm down for a movie. What are we watching?"

"Ladies choice. Go to the controller over there and scroll through the movie titles. Click enter when you find one you want."

"All right."

There are several rows of seats in their home theatre, but they select the three seats in the front. Saving me the one in the middle. I decide on a *Jason Bourne* marathon which seems a win-win for everyone. I get to watch Matt Damon kick ass and they get to watch Matt Damon kick ass. We're just watching for different reasons. By the middle of the second movie, Camden's hand is on my thigh, and he's slowly rubbing it back and forth.

I don't say anything but just try to continue eating my popcorn.

He politely takes the popcorn bag out of my hand and puts it on the seat next to him. Then he presses a button on my chair that extends the chair into a laid back lounge position. My head is back. My legs up. And by the next scene his hand is dangerously close to making its way in between my legs.

I still don't say anything.

Eventually his hand lands on my heated mound. Kneading and massaging me into a totally heightened state. My legs begin to part on their own, and it isn't until one of my legs touches Cutter's that I realize what I was doing. I'm letting Cam touch me with his brother right next to me. Did they lace the butter on this popcorn with something?

"Wait—"

Camden stops moving his hand.

"You all right?" he asks gently.

"I just want to be clear, and no disrespect, but I'm not letting Cutter touch me. I don't get down like that."

"Understood, bean." Cutter agrees. "I just want you to feel good on whatever terms you're comfortable with. I'm fine with just watching."

I've always been very comfortable with my body. Hell, I walk around my apartment naked all of the time. But I've never had sex or been sexual with someone else in the room. That is just pushing all sorts of control boundaries for me.

"I thought you didn't like sharing?" I ask Camden.

"Cutter is the exception."

Camden turns my head to face him making sure to be extra careful with me. He slides his tongue inside of my mouth and begins a languid exploration of my mouth.

Teasing my tongue with soft suction and taking soft bites of my lip.

"Her mouth tastes like red licorice and hot butter, Cut."

"Yeah?"

Camden continues kissing me as the hand that was between my legs slides up and under my shirt. Cupping one of my breasts, kneading it gently, and playing with my nipple.

"No bra," he announces.

Is he going to give Cutter a play-by-play of everything he does to me? It's actually kind of hot. I don't mind it.

Camden stops kissing me and tells me to, "Lie back and let my brother watch while I make you come for me, Jade."

Fuck.

When I turn my head to look at Cutter, his eyes bore into mine with a hunger I've never seen before. I can almost feel the floor drop from beneath me. He's using a slow and deliberate pace while he rubs a very large erection inside of his sweats. If he were to speak, I'd swear he would be asking me permission to pull it out. For me to taste it. Or maybe that's what I'm fantasizing he'll say.

Camden pinches my nipple firmly and everything down south clenches in delight. My mouth opens but nothing comes out but an indiscernible sound.

"Taste." Cutter demands gruffly.

Camden leans completely on his side facing me and takes his hand and slides it completely down the front of my leggings.

"No panties."

"Fuck," Cutter groans. Stroking himself harder.

Camden slowly begins sinking one of his fingers inside of me.

Then two.

"Soaking wet," he reports.

"Taste," Cutter demands more urgently this time.

Camden slides his finger in and out of me several more times while flicking my clit rapidly back and forth with his thumb. I start lifting my hips urging him on. Begging for more. Everything inside of me begins to wind and coil tightly, and then I start to shudder as my orgasm glides over me. My pussy clenching his finger tightly. In the middle of my release, Camden pulls his finger completely out, smacks my pussy with three fingers, and I convulse again and again.

All I can do at this point is whimper in exhaustion when he slides all three fingers into my mouth with instructions. "Taste yourself, Jade. This is what you taste like when I'm in between your legs. You see why I always want more? You taste so fucking good."

My eyes begin to close in bliss as I suck, and taste myself on his fingers.

"Eyes open," Cutter demands.

On command I flick them open, and when I do Cutter grins in approval. Continuing the deliberate, hard strokes of his cock.

I inadvertently lick my lips. Imagining the taste again.

Camden notices my reaction and chuckles. "Are you sure you don't want Cutter to play?"

I don't give a verbal answer, and I don't nod yes or no. Honestly I'm not sure about anything that's happening right now. I just know it feels good. Everything they're doing feels good.

The brothers look silently at each other, and then Camden gives Cutter a single head nod. Almost instantaneously, Cutter stops stroking himself, leans over, and gives me a gentle kiss. Making sure to swipe his entire tongue inside of my mouth.

"You taste delicious, bean. Exactly like I knew you would," Cutter says. "Do you trust me?"

I nod my head yes, but I'm scared.

"We're just going to make you feel good." Camden promises as he waits for my consent. "Nothing you can't handle."

"Okay," I whisper nervously.

Cutter sits up and walks behind my chair. He crouches down behind my head and stretches my arms up by the sides of my head. Pulling my shirt up and off.

"Hold onto my head while I kiss you. I want to taste you again. Don't move those hands."

Cutter bends over and starts kissing me passionately, while I hold onto his head. At the same time, he uses his hands to starts playing with my breasts. Massaging and kneading them. Rolling my nipples with his knuckles and fingertips. Over and over until my breathing becomes labored.

Then Camden stands in front of me.

When he starts to pull my leggings completely off I panic a little. It was a knee jerk reaction. I stop kissing Cutter back and motion to keep my leggings on, when I hear a sharp command by my ear. "Don't move those hands."

Camden stands there watching us. Waiting for my reaction. I consider what I'm doing and who I'm doing it with. Two men I trust. Two men who would risk everything for me. Who I would risk everything for. One man who I think I may be falling in love with.

And that's when I decide to finally let go.

CAMDEN

I'm taking a moment to appreciate the view. To witness the initial trepidation then complete surrender of a beautiful woman I have always cared for and now adore. I imagine that I'm breaking every one of her rules, and practically destroying the walls of safety that she's erected around her heart. Even though she seems to be enjoying it physically, this has got to be difficult for her, but I'm honored and humbled that she would give herself over to me in this way.

When Jade places her hands back on my brother's head upon his command, Cutter lifts his eyes to mine in appreciation and gratitude as well. He knows that this probably won't be commonplace. That I'm not likely to share my bed on a regular basis with him, and not just because Jade may not be able to handle that or want that, but because I probably won't want it either.

But I also realize that Cutter was scared shitless too. Scared that we almost lost Jade to that maniac, Chase. Frightened that she could have been seriously injured on our watch. Another mistake that we'd have to pay the highest price for. Thankfully, yet again, my brother was there when I needed him to be. He saved our asses when we were almost shot in the head after the casino fiasco, and he saved us once again, because he was able to handle Chase Whitman before the guy was able to do any real damage to our girl.

I know we don't take tabs, keep score, or owe each other favors. Ever. We're brothers. But I can't forget what he's done for me. If I had lost Jade, I would have probably lost myself to the anger, the guilt, and the pain that would have consumed me. He saved me, and in doing so, he saved us. So I won't deny him what he needs so badly right now. What we both need.

Comfort.

Release.

Domination.

Jade.

I wait patiently as Cutter starts to seduce Jade with his mouth again. Her hands remain over her head as he softly runs his fingertips around the circumference of her nipples. Her tight, flat stomach begins to rise and fall with increased speed. Her hips start to wiggle and her feet start to rub each other in angst. As I watch her desire build, I know what I want to do now. This is my show to direct and direct it I will.

"Put your mouth on her tits, Cutter."

Cutter lifts his head and moves farther over Jade's body. He takes heavy possession of one of her breasts with his mouth. Carefully grazing his teeth around her nipple. I watch in proud approval as she gradually begins panting for breath.

"You should be able to touch him now, Jade. Reach in and grab Cutter's dick. Jerk him off."

I painfully walk over to her, having to manage my own

brick hard erection, and gently start rubbing my palm against her stomach. Talking to her in assured tones.

"That's it, baby. You're doing fucking fantastic. Cutter loves it. I'm so proud of you."

I hear a soft whimper from the back of her throat as I bend down and begin to pepper soft kisses against her stomach, her hips, her mound, and all around her labia. Being sure to purposely avoid her clit. I'm saving that for last.

Cutter moves his mouth to Jade's other breast with more determination than before. Taking stronger pulls. Tonguing her nipple down harder. I can tell he's about to explode, but he's trying to hold off.

"Harder, Jade," I order.

"Uhhhh—" she grunts with wild abandonment.

She's about to come too.

I figure it's time I give them both the release they desperately need.

"Come for me, Jade," I demand as I grip under her ass with both hands, and bury my head between her legs and suck.

"Aaah!" she screams in blissful surrender and it's the most beautiful capitulation I think I've ever heard. Cutter comes all over the floor and himself in a loud grunt. I pop my head up to watch them both, as I continue to massage Jade's pussy with light strokes.

Satisfied with my handiwork, I need to take care of myself before I spontaneously combust.

"Switch," I command.

Cutter pulls his sweats up and switches places with me. Grabbing one of the drinks from earlier, he takes a quick sip, then he reaches his hand in and pulls out a few small ice cubes. Placing them directly in between Jade's legs and diving his head in to swirl them around his mouth and her pussy before they all melt from the heat.

"Oh my God!" she yelps.

"Look at me, Jade," I command.

I'm kneeling by her head. When she turns it, she sees me stroking myself. My angry erection jutting forth, waiting to be put out of its misery.

She stares hungrily at me.

Then at Cutter.

Trying to decide which distraction to pay attention to.

"Eyes on me, baby," I tell her.

"Yes," she moans.

Without me asking she lifts her hands towards me, pulling me closer, and inviting me in and down her throat. I watch with utter adoration as she takes me farther inside of her mouth, inch by exquisite inch, sucking me harder every time Cutter sucks her harder.

"Her cunt tastes like lemon icing," Cutter comments after coming up for air.

"She tastes like heaven," I growl in response as my eyes roll back in my head.

I've been hard for at least twenty minutes, so it doesn't take long for me to burst in her mouth, and I watch delightedly as she swallows every last drop. When she's finished, I tuck myself back into my shorts and bend down to start kissing her. I want to make sure I swallow every bit of her orgasm when Cutter takes her over the top. She's already very close to the edge, but I want to pull her back from the precipice for a moment.

"Motor," I instruct Cutter. Then I return back to kissing Jade.

Cutter stands up and walks over to the built in toy chest we have in the theatre and takes his sweet old time picking out a toy for us to play with. Toys are Cutter's thing. So I indulge him, and get lost inside of Jade's sweet mouth while I wait. When he walks back over, he's carrying two of his favorite toys, with a wicked grin on his face. I shake my head. A dildo for stuffing and a vibrator for clit play. Jade may pass out before it's all over.

"You're so wet, Jade, this is going to slip right inside of you," Cutter says excitedly.

I like to watch, so I lift my head to watch Cutter work his magic, while holding Jade's arms back above her head. A bit of tension will help heighten the experience for her.

As he works the dildo inside of her, twisting and pushing, Jade tilts her hips up. Yearning and begging for more.

Cutter laughs out loud. "She loves it, Cam."

"You love it right, baby?" I ask her.

She's overcome with sensations and it's hard for her to respond, but I need to hear the words.

"You love it right, Jade?" I ask again.

"Should I get the clamps?" Cutter asks almost chomping at the bit.

"No, I'll use my mouth."

I bend down and blow gently on one of Jade's nipples. We've been playing with them for a while now, so I know they must be slightly tender, but just the right amount of pressure will be what she needs to get verbal. After several more swirls of my tongue and a few more soft blows, I bite.

The sensation zings right to her core, because her lips lift, and Cutter is able to finish up working the dildo as far in as she can take.

I release.

I can hear soft mews coming from her now. So I ask her again.

"You love what we're doing, Jade, or are you ready to stop?"

"Fuckers!" she exclaims.

"Stop or go?" I say again almost laughing. Already knowing the answer. She's cussing us out because she wants to come so badly she could spit nails.

"GO!"

As soon as she gives the word, my mouth descends back on her other nipple, and Cutter turns his special ordered Hitachi vibrator on low. He presses the vibrator against her clit ramping her pleasure up and up and up.

Then he pulls it away.

"If you're a good girl, Jade, one day me and my brother will fill you up and stretch you wide and work that pussy and that ass, side to side, and front to back, until you beg us to stop. Good girls get the Kings anywhere and everywhere they want, for as long as they can stand it," Cutter taunts. Knowing his promise of more to come will get her higher and higher.

"Please—" she begs softly.

Cutter looks at me with question, but I shake my head no. Jade's begging for release, not for us to fill her every orifice. She's not ready for that. He looks disappointed by my response, but stays focused on the task at hand. Turning the Hitachi up a notch, he presses it again to her clit. Carefully watching her response and knowing just when to pull it back.

"Dammit!" she yells.

"I swallow her agony with my mouth then use my hand to start working the dildo in and out of her."

Her hips working to meet my every stroke.

She's so fucking responsive.

It's a beautiful thing to watch.

I'm a lucky man.

I give Cutter one last head nod. She's ready to blow. I keep my mouth on hers, while still working the dildo in and out of her, and then Cutter turns the knob one notch higher on the vibrator and places it on her clit.

And holds it there.

Everything inside of Jade swirls and tightens like there's fire traveling through her veins.

Her hips jut straight up.

Her nails feel like sharp talons as they dig into the skin of my arms.

Her pussy clamps down on the dildo so tightly she almost swallows it whole. I can't believe I'm actually jealous of a dildo.

And her face.

Her face looks like it's experiencing the most pleasurable pain known to man, and I feel like the proudest peacock on the planet that I help put that look there.

The credits are rolling and the room is silent except for the fact that all three of us sound like we just ran a race. We're breathing heavily, on our backs, sprawled out on the chairs. Especially Jade. I consider for a moment that perhaps I pushed her too hard tonight. She did just suffer a trauma. All this stimulation can't be good for her head, but she hasn't complained. Not once. Although she hasn't looked at either of us in the last few minutes.

Shit, I think we spooked her.

Being pleasured by two men can be overwhelming for a novice. Especially by us. I clasp her hand with mine.

"Are you okay?"

"Yes."

"I mean are you okay with what just happened in here?"

"Yes, I'm—"

"I'm going to start dinner, okay?" Cutter interrupts. Gracefully exiting to give us a moment.

I nod okay.

"Come here," I say to Jade, patting my lap.

Jade climbs up and into my embrace.

"Tell me about yesterday."

"What about it?"

"Tell me why you didn't tell anyone about Chase."

"Well, I think I underestimated his crazy."

"Cutter said he'd been watching you for days, maybe weeks, in his car? That's kind of crazy in my book."

I kiss the back of her hand. Wanting her to understand that I'm not angry, just concerned. She lays her head against my chest. Tracing one of my crown tattoos with her pointer finger. The origin of the tat is a long story featuring my brother and two bottles of scotch when I turned twenty-one.

"I do so much work for you guys. I know how to run intel. I thought I could handle it."

"But you couldn't have run intel on him, Jade. You would have seen that he was a cop a long time ago, or did you know that already?"

"I admit, I didn't do a *deep* search. I just watched him for a while. He was quiet. He didn't bother me. I thought maybe—"

"You thought wrong and as many years as you've worked for us, you should know better. No one ever knows better than the collective. You tell the group what's going on, and then we make a decision together on how to handle it."

"We don't make decisions together. You all make the decisions. I just follow orders."

"That's not true, Jade. Roman practically had you managing his entire life at one point. Cutter and I always ask for your input and your guidance. We trust you like no other woman except for maybe our mother. God rest her soul."

"Okay."

"Don't ever scare us like that again. I knew something was

going on with you and if something had … I'm just saying that if something had, it would have been a bad scene."

"Okay."

"And poor Roman, he's fucking livid. Chase was using you as bait to draw him out. You better give him a call tomorrow to assure him that his favorite tiny terror is just fine. I've put him on a time out for now, but he's not going to stand for it too much longer."

She chuckles. "Okay."

"Come closer." I say as she burrows herself further into me.

"Cam—"

"Yes, baby."

"I don't want to manage the club anymore."

I chuckle. "One gun to the head and you're bailing on me?"

"I want you to teach me to do what you do."

"Are you crazy—"

Jades hand starts to slide up my chest and around my neck.

"I want thirty days," she murmurs.

"What?" I ask as I wrap some of her hair around my fist. Giving me better access to marking her neck with my mouth. I'm not above giving her a hickey to mark my property.

"Give me thirty days," she moans as I gently suck her sweet lemon scented skin. "Teach me everything you know … and then we'll see how it goes."

I start kissing the side of her face. So fucking happy by how she's turning my own words back around on me. And even happier as she hops off of me and starts working my basketball shorts down.

This is her show to run, and I happily allow her to do so.

She pushes the button on the chair, sitting it in the upright position as I start to stroke myself.

"Let me help you with that," she says as she bends on both knees and takes me in her mouth.

Evidently Jade loves fellatio.

And I love that she loves it.

She pulls up hard on my dick and swirls her tongue around my tip. Sampling some of the precum dripping from the slit.

"I probably should've asked before I put your dick in my mouth, but are you clean?"

I smile. "Yes, just tested last month. Are you?"

"Funny since your mouth has been all in my pussy, but yes."

"On birth control?"

"Yes," she answers with a fire in her eyes that excites me.

"Then I think you should have a seat."

Jade climbs up on top of me, and I make sure to slide a bit forward so her legs can fit on either side of me in the chair. When she begins her slow, torturous descent on my cock, I groan like a bitch. When I'm completely seated inside of her she stops moving for a moment to get adjusted to the girth of me. It's never an easy fit when I'm fucking her. She's narrowly built, and tight as shit, but the pleasure is in the journey. She might sit like that for an hour if I don't move things along. So I grasp her hips and start to rock them forward and back.

"Like this, baby."

She grabs my head and neck, her breasts directly in front of my mouth, and I start nipping and teasing them as she begins to move her hips on her own accord.

"Fuck, Jade, that feels so good."

I want to laugh when I hear a couple of pots clanking extra loudly in the kitchen. Cutter's pouting. When he peeps his head in to watch, I nod for him to come over. Since I've come once already, I could fuck Jade all night if need be. After the first orgasm, my stamina is legendary. So now it's back to taking care of her pleasure.

Cutter keeps his distance, watching as she rides the fuck out of me. Stroking his hard on and biting his lip. I grab Jade by the waist and hips and roughly pull her up and off of me, quickly pivoting her around so that she's riding me cowgirl style. Facing Cutter. Then I help her work her way back down my engorged dick again. Slowly. It's a completely different feeling when she's in this position and I want to be sure I'm careful with what's mine.

"Grab your tits, Jade," Cutter commands.

Her eyes on his.

His eyes on hers.

My face buried in her hair.

My brother is theatrical. So he cuts the movie screen off, puts the satellite radio on which is playing a deep house mix, and he turns the strobe lights on.

"You're fucking beautiful, Jade. Ride Cam to the beat of the song. A little faster."

She works me faster.

Loving the mixture of the hypnotic music, the lights, and my dick inside of her.

"Yes—just like that," he approves.

Jade arches her back and holds onto me from behind. She can't take too much more. I can feel her pussy clamping. Her body trembling. I whisper by her ear.

"Whose pussy is this?"

Her breathing grows heavier.

She's riding me harder.

Cutter is coming.

"Tell me before my brother comes all over himself again."

She groans.

"Yours."

"Whose?"

"Yours!" she yells. Coming and laughing simultaneously.

"All hail to the king!" she exclaims as she flops her body against me.

Yes, I say to myself.

She finally fucking gets it.

She's mine.

It takes me an entire twenty-four hours, before I can look Cutter King directly in his face again. After our night of debauchery in the movie room, I took to Camden's bed and stayed there, under the covers. The boys both cut me some slack though and decided to let me come to acceptance of what we had shared on my own.

I spend another three days at the King house, but Cutter doesn't touch me or watch us have sex again. In fact, half of the time he isn't there. So Camden spends most of our time together feeding me, fucking me, and teaching me the basics of how to read computer code.

It's on the fourth day of my King slumber party that my sister frantically calls me.

"Jade!"

"What is it?"

"Where the hell have you been?"

My naughty little king hid my cell phone and only gave it back to me today.

"I'm sorry," I say scrolling through my missed calls. Shit, there's like twenty of them. "I dropped my phone in the toilet. It took me a couple of days to dry it out in some rice," I lie.

"Don't you make enough money to buy a new phone?"

"Why would I do that when I can just dry it out? Listen, that's not the point of this call. What was so important?"

"And when your phone was stuck in this bowl of rice, did you go live somewhere else too?"

"What?"

"I went by your place more than once. You haven't been there in days."

Busted.

"Okay, I'm over at a friend's house."

"So you finally made some headway with the twin I take it."

Camden's working at his desk on his computer, but I know he's listening to every word I say. I think the boys have seen Jana all of maybe three times. There's no way I wanted those two worlds to collide.

"That's not it, Jana," I huff. "Could you please just tell me what's wrong."

"I'm in trouble."

"What kind of trouble?"

"The bank wants to take the house."

"What house?"

"Our house."

"Dad's house?" I ask incredulously.

"Yes, Jade. Our childhood home."

"So let 'em take it."

"What? Our mother made a life for us in that house."

"Houses are just bricks. Home is where you make it."

"Oh would you cut the Hallmark bullshit. Dad's going to be out on his ass if we don't do something."

"He's a grown ass man. Can't he handle it?"

"Obviously not."

"Jana—"

"I know what you're thinking, but this isn't me trying to manipulate you into seeing Dad. You don't even need to talk to him if you don't want. This is about us doing what Mom would want us to do. She loved him, and she loved that house."

"All this from someone who barely remembers her voice."

"That's a low blow, Jade, even for you."

I sigh.

"You're right. I'm sorry. What do you need me to do?"

"Speak with the mortgage company. See if there's some last rabbit we can pull out of a hat to save the house. I spoke to them a couple of times but they were reluctant to talk numbers and specifics with me, because my name's not on the house."

"Neither is mine."

"No but you're Dad's power of attorney."

"What? No I'm not."

"You are. I've seen the paperwork. It was drawn up years ago."

"When?"

"When you were living with Tyson."

"That's crazy. Can you just do that? Just draw up a power of attorney without telling the person?"

Camden turns his head to look at me.

"I guess you can when it's your family."

"All right. I'm not promising anything, Jana. I've got drama of my own to deal with. I don't need his shit too."

"Just make a few calls."

"I'll let you know what happens."

"Okay."

. . .

After I hang up the phone, I stare at it for a moment. Quiet and reflective.

"You know you have to actually get your hands on a physical copy of that POA to use it. Companies are going to want you to fax it over before they deal with you. They're not just going to take your word for it," Camden says.

"What."

"You're going to have to go get it from your father."

"No wait, I'll call Jana back."

"No, Jade. What are you afraid of? He can't hurt you anymore. He's just a broken down old man who's losing his house. I'll come with you if you want."

"You will?"

"I'm offended you even have to question that."

"Because I fucked your brains out for a week?" I grin.

"No, baby, because I've made it perfectly clear that you belong to me, and I take care of what's mine."

"I like it when you call me baby." I tease as I climb him like a tree.

"Careful, Jade. This chair is old."

"I said I like it when you call me baby. Not Jade."

"You do, huh?" He smiles at my playfulness.

"Yep. It's so much better than itty bitty, or munchkin, or tiny terror, or lima bean, or tiny tot or—"

"I get it. You're sick of the short jokes."

"Elementary, Watson!" I throw my hand up.

"Then come here, baby."

And Camden pulls me in for a long kiss that ends when we both fall out of his wobbly desk chair and onto the floor laughing hysterically.

~

My anxiety builds as Camden drives to my old neighborhood. He's adorable though, because he's trying everything to make me relax. Talk about someone not liking having no control over a situation. He hates that not I'm smiling, or laughing, or busting his balls. I'm just quiet, and he can't stand a quiet Jade.

"So you grew up about twenty minutes from us." He tries again at making conversation.

"Uh-huh."

"I never did get the story of how you and Roman met. You were wrapped up with the drug addict really young right? So it couldn't have been a romantic connection."

Look at him digging for gold.

"Your best friend never told you the story? I find that hard to believe."

"We don't talk about shit like that, Jade. We just talk about money."

"Really? He wasn't like *I hit that the other night*," I say in my best Roman impersonation.

"What the fuck!" My king roars. "I specifically asked that bastard."

"You're so easy." I chuckle.

"That's not funny, Jade."

"Okay, okay. I'll tell you the story. It's not a big deal honestly. I was at a party when I was seventeen. I was there with Tyson. These were his friends, so while he got high with them, I was mostly relegated to kitchen duty. Keeping things clean. Making sure no one was sticking roofies in the girls' drinks."

"Nice."

"I know, he was a shitty boyfriend, but I didn't know any differently. He was my first one."

"I'm your first boyfriend."

"Okay, King Kong, *you're* my first."

"So continue."

"So anyway, the party was getting out of hand. Everyone was high. The music was loud. The house was trashed. Typical party for those days. Then two guys got in an argument right outside of the house. Total stoners. A knife was drawn and one of them was stabbed in the side. I saw it through the window. I'll never forget it. The kid who was stabbed was wearing a white wife beater shirt. He fell immediately to the ground. Clutching his stomach. I could see a pool of red blood forming on his side through the shirt. I thought for sure he was dead."

"Fucked up."

"Yeah, turn on this block, Cam. It's a shortcut."

"Okay."

"So anyway, the neighbors must have called the cops, and people started scattering. I went looking for Tyson but I couldn't find him. I thought that he might have been slouched in a corner somewhere high, so I continued to look for him in the house. It never dawned on me that he left me there."

"Damn."

"Exactly. So when the police came I was still in the house like an idiot. They took me and a couple of other people in for questioning. Roman just happened to be at the station for something. I never knew what. He was talking himself out of something, throwing Joseph's name around as leverage, but I could see that they were going for it. I thought maybe Joseph was a high-powered lawyer or something, so I did the same thing with the woman questioning me. They gave me a female cop thinking I'd cooperate better. I told her a little of what I saw which I could tell she didn't really believe. So then I decided to tell her that Joseph Masterson was my stepfather, and that he would back my story, and that immediately made her stop writing her report."

"He definitely knows a lot of people. His name rings bell in low circles."

"What's your deal with him?"

"I think he knows something about my father's murder."

"Really? No offense, but I thought your father dealt in petty crime."

"Joseph wasn't always who he is."

"So you worked for a man you thought had something do with your dad's murder?"

"I only recently found this out. That's why I wanted us on our own. There's nothing I can do about it now, but I certainly didn't want to continue making money for the prick."

"Wow."

"Don't say anything to Roman, okay?"

"What about the whole *we're a collective* speech you gave me?"

"This is the only thing I'll ask you to keep from him. No matter how much shit Rome talks about the old man, Joseph is his father. His blood. It will change things between us if we tell him."

"Cutter knows."

"Cutter knows everything."

"Oh right, he did tell me you two were interchangeable."

"Did he?"

"He did."

"Well, not with everything." He chuckles.

"No, not with everything."

"So go on. You said Joseph was your stepdad. Ballsy move with the son in the building."

"Exactly, it was definitely a hail Mary, but it worked. She told her superior, who pulled Roman to the side and asked him about it. Roman came over to me and gave an Oscar worthy performance. *'So you're my father's other kid I've been hearing about?'"*

"Hilarious."

"Yeah and luckily I overheard his earlier conversation, so I knew his first name. So I said, 'Yes, Roman, I'm your baby sis.' It was a priceless performance. It took everything for me not to use my Darth Vader voice."

"You're nuts."

"And that was it. He got me out of there, and we've been thicker than thieves ever since. He would take me out to eat for my birthday some years. He'd check in on me once he discovered how much of a loser Tyson was, and then when the fights started escalating between us, is when I think he decided he was going to pull me out of there. By hook or by crook."

"Yeah, I don't think we were leaving that apartment without you agreeing to working for him and leaving that loser. It wasn't optional. He was just making it sound like it was."

"You thought I was a complete nut job."

"I did and I still do. I'm no bed of roses to live with either. You have to be a bit touched in the head to deal with a King."

"We're here," I announce flatly. "The small one over there with the overgrown bushes."

Camden parallel parks in front of my childhood home as I look at the dead grass, overgrown bushes, and crumbling steps.

"My mother is rolling over in her grave," I say somberly.

"No she's not. She's happy that you're here. Let's go, chipmunk."

"That didn't last long. You're back to your lame short jokes."

"Oops that was a slip. You're going to have to give me a minute to get used to using only terms of endearment that you approve of. It's not in my nature to be so accommodating."

"Oh, forget it. Let's go and get this shit over with."

I turn my palm over, and he grabs it with his own.

As we climb the steps I notice a bulge under the back of Camden's shirt.

"What's that?"

"My piece."

"You brought a gun to my father's house?"

"You think I'm going to take any chances with you ever again? I don't give a shit that he's your father. You two are estranged. He may have gone bat shit crazy in there. Hell, I don't know. What I do know is that I never go into a situation that I can't control unprepared. Are we on the same page?"

"Understood."

"Good, then ring the bell."

JADE

I'm doing something that I never thought I'd be doing in a zillion years. I'm meeting my sister for dinner with my new boyfriend, *the twin,* (as she continues to call him) in tow. We're meeting at one of her favorite places, so she won't gripe about the service or the quality of the food. A quaint American eatery near the Art Museum.

She's been babbling on for the last ten minutes about the students in her eight o'clock class and how they're a better group of students than her ten o'clock group. Blah, blah, blah. I'm bored already, so I know Camden has to be too. He's sitting here though, sipping on his scotch, and nodding his head at the appropriate times.

"Sorry to change the subject," she says as if we were listening to the original subject, "but I just wanted to let you know that the bank has agreed to put dad in the home retention program."

"Yeah, I got the approval letter a few days ago," I say.

"Oh, they send you a copy of the letters too I guess."

"Yeah."

"So I didn't ask you before, because I thought it would be

too soon, but what did he say to you? Was he … civil at least?"

"He was nothing like I remembered."

"Really?"

"He cried and he gave me a hug. He thanked me for helping him and then he spent the next thirty minutes of our visit trying to find those damn papers. I didn't think the power of attorney existed for a minute."

I can see that Jana is dying to tell me, *I told you so*, but she's holding back for once in her life. Maybe we'll be able to figure out this sister thing after all. It's what my mother would have wanted. It's what I want. I love my sister. I always have. I just need to remember that sometimes.

"How long has he been sober?" I ask her.

"About three years. As soon as he heard about the cancer."

"He really needs to go into a hospice care facility, Jana."

"He wants to die at home, in the bed that he shared with Mom."

I roll my eyes. Sure I let the man give me a hug, but I'm not about to get all sentimental about him wanting to feel close to my mother. He barely held her hand when she was on her deathbed. He's still a bastard in my eyes.

"Did he apologize to you?" Jana asks.

"In his way."

Camden takes another sip of his scotch, because we're leaving out the part where he told me that I remember things a lot differently than he does. As if I was lying or mentally unstable, and he wasn't verbally and mentally abusive.

"So, Jana, why don't you tell me something about you other than those students of yours." Camden tries to make conversation.

"All she does is work, Cam. She has a ten year plan or something."

"Fifteen year plan," Jana corrects me. "It will work too if Professor Owens doesn't sabotage me."

"Professor Owens?" he asks.

"Yeah, he's the guy I'm a teaching assistant for."

"Is he bothering you? You want me to have a talk with him?"

"No!" she blurts out quickly. "I mean I don't need him roughed up or anything," she whispers so the restaurant won't think she's ordering a mob hit.

"Oh, okay." Camden chortles.

I tilt my head for a moment and look at my sister.

"Jana, are you sleeping with your professor?"

"What?! Absolutely not."

"Do you *like* him?"

"No, Jade, of course not."

Huh. I wonder.

"So, Camden, how did you get my sister to go on a date with you after all of this time? She seemed so dead set against it."

I give her a look of death.

"Dead set against it, huh?" Camden leans back in his chair, legs spread, and licks a droplet of scotch off of his mouth. "Fuck, he looks delicious. "Well, I'm very persuasive when I want to be."

Jana looks between us with a satisfied smile.

"Well it's a good thing you are. I've never seen her happier."

Ugh, this girl.

"Jade why aren't you drinking? OH MY GOD! Are you pregnant?" My sister's decibel level goes from ten to one when she says the word pregnant. Again so the restaurant won't think that she's sitting with an unwed mother.

"Are you on crack? No. I'm just taking it easy lately," I say.

"Oh, because I'm too young to be someone's aunt."

I roll my eyes.

"I know, Jana. Don't worry. You're safe for a real long time."

~

"So what did you think about my sister?" I ask Camden as I sit on his bed peeling off my clothes.

"She was amusing."

"That's it? Amusing?"

"Okay if you need more, she's a bit uppity, and an education snob, but she loves you. So I like her."

"What else?"

"I think she has the hots for her professor."

"You do?! Me too!"

Camden walks into the bathroom and checks the water for the shower.

"Is it hot?" I call out.

"Yeah, it's good. Come on."

I lean against the shower wall as Camden rubs my shoulders. The water feels good as it beats down on the two of us.

"This is a big shower," I say. "Bigger than Roman's even."

"Uh, huh."

"Big men like big showers or something?"

"Something like that."

I turn around to look my new lover in the eyes. Camden's hard to read, but I'm learning more about him every day. He's being particularly evasive.

"Something like that?"

"Everyone has their own reasons for liking what they like, Jade. Roman has his reasons. I

have mine. But since you brought it up, let's get it out on the table."

"Okay."

"You've been hiding from Cutter for days."

"Not hiding."

"Hiding. You're hurting his feelings."

I turn my lips up. "Really? I doubt that."

"He's worried that you hate him."

"Of course I don't."

"Are you freaked out about what happened?"

"A little."

"What about it exactly?"

"I don't know if I could ever do what, you know, what he was talking about you two would do to me if I was good."

"He was just trying to turn you on."

"But you have done that before? With other women?"

"Yes."

"Are you always this honest?"

"Always," he smiles.

"In this shower? Was that the whole point you were trying to avoid? You have a big shower so three people can fit inside of it easily." I roll my eyes.

"I know we're not getting sensitive about past lovers, because I think you may be the only woman who has a list to rival mine."

"That's not even close to the truth!"

Camden laughs out loud.

"Seriously though, Cutter and I will only do what you're comfortable with. If you decide you never want him in the room again, then he won't be."

"You won't be mad?"

"No, Jade. This relationship is just us. Cutter is only a secondary character."

"And if I want him to ... play again?"

"That's fine too. You set the ground rules. We will abide by them."

"Okay."

"So will you talk to him now?"

"Yes, I will. I'm sorry. I was being a punk."

"It's okay that you're attracted to Cutter you know. There's nothing wrong with it. I don't live in some bubble where I think you'll never look at another man, and of course it makes total sense that you're attracted to someone who looks a lot like me."

"Oh, brother."

"Just as long as you know that at the end of the day that you belong to me, Jade. All thirty-day contracts have been nullified. This is a lifetime assignment. I love you. You will *always* belong to me.

I smile. Almost blushing.

"And this belongs to me."

He touches my mouth.

"And these belong to me."

My breasts.

"And this."

He thrusts a finger inside of me.

I close my eyes for a moment from the sudden pleasurable intrusion. Then I raise my arms up as a signal for him to lift me up. He pulls out of me and lifts me up. I wrap my legs tightly around his waist as he begins to devour my mouth. When he pulls back his head, he slides his finger into my mouth.

"Taste."

I stare deeply into his eyes as I lick every drop of me off of him. When he finally pulls his finger free, I initiate the next kiss. A tear rolls down my face while I do. Luckily we're in the shower, under the spray, and he doesn't see it.

Yes, I've become one of *those* girls.

I'm picturing a forever after with him.

I want to buy a pink toothbrush and put it in the holder next to his.

I want to hold his hand on every flight he has to take.

I'm so happy, that I'm scared shitless.

But like my man said, it's all right to live life experiencing a healthy dose of fear.

Because that's how you know that you're really living.

EPILOGUE

CAMDEN

"Hey."

"Hey, yourself," Cutter casually responds. Not turning his head toward me; typing away at something on yet another one of my burner laptops. "Where have you been all day?" he casually asks.

"It's moving day tomorrow, asshole, so I was helping the little one pack."

"Oh shit, that's right."

"*Oh shit, that's right*," I parrot back with loads of attitude in my voice.

My all of a sudden absentminded brother was supposed to meet me at Jade's apartment over two hours ago to help me box up and tape the contents of her kitchen cabinets. I kick off my boots and hang my jacket on the hook by the door.

"You haven't changed your mind about Jade moving in here have you?"

He finally stops typing and swivels around in the chair.

"Why would I do that?"

"I don't know. It will be a big change for us."

"Yeah, a change for the better. She cooks better than you. She works out harder than you. She definitely smells better than you. And best of all, we get to play with her all over the house anytime we want now."

"That's not funny."

"Do you see me laughing?"

"You do realize we aren't going to be sharing my woman twenty-four seven right?"

"Obviously, asshole," Cutter snickers. "I've got my own woman to claim. I don't need yours too."

I look over Cutter's shoulder and take a peek at the screen of the laptop. Now I see why he never showed up. He's scrolling through web images of the glamazon. At this point I think it's become an obsession. Like masturbating.

"I'll bite," I say fed up, helping myself to some of the Thai leftovers in the fridge. "Tell me what you're doing, so that I can help, and so that you can finally be finished with this ridiculous project of yours."

"It's an ongoing thing. There's not much you can do to *finish* it."

"Ongoing?"

"Yeah ... convincing the glamazon, *I mean Sloan*, to see the light is going to be a little more difficult for me than it was for you. I can't just force her into working for me twenty-four hours a day. We don't have a history of a friendship like you and Jade do. I don't even think she likes me. It's going to take a bit more finesse for me to get the job done."

"And what's your motivation? I'm really trying to understand. I mean she is definitely beautiful. I would assume she's not a gold digger since she comes from money, but that describes a thousand privileged socialites up and down the East Coast. Some we've shared together in this house."

"I didn't say it made sense."

"So the plan is to …"

"The plan is to cut all possible suitors out of her life until she comes to her senses about me."

I have to laugh out loud. "Cutter, have you lost your mind? When's the last time you even saw her? I don't think the woman even gives two shits about you."

"When has a woman ever said no to me? Even yours."

I throw a glass of iced tea at his head.

Quick little fucker ducks just in the nick of time.

"Good try!" He chuckles. "But I'm faster than you, big brother."

"Go clean it up, and watch your fucking mouth about my girlfriend. I'm going to marry that woman. She only said yes to you because I told her to."

"Keep telling yourself that."

"You know what, you're on your own! I can't wait to see how this shit blows up in your face."

"Yee of little faith. I've got this one, Cam. I'll bet you a thousand dollars and a breakfast that your girlfriend has to cook for me in only her bra and panties."

"You've lost your fucking mind if you think I'm involving Jade in any juvenile wager with you."

"That's what I thought."

He turns around and starts scrolling through some more pictures of Sloan. I pour myself another glass of iced tea and silently finish my plate of lime chicken watching him. After I finish eating, I toss my plate in the sink and hover over his shoulder.

"Can I help you?" he asks nonchalantly.

"Just the money," I agree to. "One grand."

"Nope, I need more motivation than that. Breakfast by Jade and one grand. That's the wager."

From what I know about her, Sloan is slick, not sweet. She's worldly, not naïve. She doesn't seem the type to have any interest in any thing long term with a certifiably crazy clown like my brother. But he's right about one thing, no woman has ever said no to him. Even when we were fucking thirteen years old. Women love him. He's the charismatic King brother, so there's definitely a chance that he could actually win this stupid bet, and then I'd really be up shit's creek. Jade would have my ass.

Of course if it doesn't work out in my favor, I could always shoot his ass.

"Bet!" I say.

Camden King was the tatted, calculated, computer hacker with a thing for his assistant Jade, but CUTTER is his wild, badass little brother who falls hard for Sloan– a woman who isn't the slightest bit interested BUT owes him big time.

Will Sloan will be able to resist the bad boy when Cutter moves in next door to collect on the debt? Will Cutter eventually win the bet he made with his brother?

Grab this sexy enemies-to-lovers romance and find out now.
DOWNLOAD INDEBTED INSTANTLY
Also Available In Print & Audio

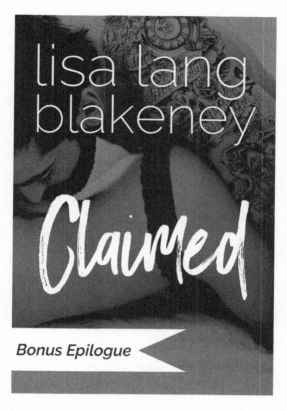

PLEASE CLICK THIS LINK TO DOWNLOAD YOUR
COPY OF THE BONUS EPILOGUE INSTANTLY

MORE BONUS STUFF!

Want access to all my bonus stuff? Read deleted scenes, character interviews, and extended epilogues for all of my releases when you visit the **Romance Ninja Room**.

CLICK FOR EXCLUSIVE ACCESS
http://lisalangblakeney.com/private-ninja-room/

BOOK LIST

The Masterson Series

Devour this addictive series about the possessive bad boy, Roman Masterson, who falls hard and fast for the girl he's promised his family to protect.

Masterson

Masterson Unleashed

Masterson In Love

Masterson Made

Joseph Loves Juliette

The King Brothers Series

Dive into this series of interconnected standalones featuring 3 alpha hot brothers and the women they lay claim to without apology.

Claimed - Camden & Jade

Indebted - Cutter & Sloan

Broken - Stone & Tiny

Promised - All King Brothers

The Nighthawk Series

Sexy & sweet sports romances set in the professional world of football. All standalones.

Saint - Saint & Sabrina

Wolf - Cooper & Ursula

Diesel - Mason & Olivia

Jett - Jett & Adrienne

Rush - Rush & Mia

The Valencia Mafia Series

Coming Soon. Get Notified!

WHERE YOU CAN FIND ME

MY VIP LIST (Get the nitty gritty)
I have a VIP Reader mailing list. I only send free books, new release, sales or special giveaway information to this group. No spam. You can join here:
http://LisaLangBlakeney.com/VIP

MY PRIVATE FAN GROUP (Casual fun)
Join my private Fan Group on Facebook also known as my "Romance Ninja Warriors" where I share all things new going on, celebrate birthdays, post teasers, yummy pics, giveaways and just chit chat.
http://LisaLangBlakeney.com/community

THE ARC TEAM (Book Reviewers)
If you are interested in joining my beta reader team then please join here: https://geni.us/N8jAU

ACKNOWLEDGMENTS

When I started writing my first book, I didn't know anyone. Not any authors, editors, or bloggers. No one. Now that this is my fifth book, I'm starting to build a team of friends and family who support me big time in this crazy world of romance publishing, for which I am so very grateful.

Thank you to my husband, Deric, my amazing 4 daughters, my mother-in-law, Noemi, as well as my besties: Erica, Tracy, Vicki, Donna, Robin, Kelly, Stacey, and Kelly J.

Thank you to my editor, Marla Esposito, my kick @ss PA, Deb Carroll, my beta reader Jessie Lynn, my street team leader, Johnnie-Marie Howard, my steadfast author mentor, Liv Morris, and new author partner in crime, Thia Finn.

A BIG thank you to all my amazing Ninja Alpha Romance Warriors and my bomb ass Street Ninjas. You ladies are amazeballs!

Huge shout out to all of the bloggers who have supported my author journey so far in any kind of way– big or small. Special shout out to blogger Crystal Grizzard Burnette of "BBB Romance Book Pimps" who does anything I ever ask of her.

Finally, I want to thank every single reader who has taken a chance on one or all of my alphas. You all are awesome! Please keep reading. My alphas demand it:)

Love Y'all,

-Lisa

ABOUT THE AUTHOR

Lisa Lang Blakeney is an international bestselling author of contemporary romance sold in more than 28 countries. Worried that her fellow PTO moms might disapprove, she wrote and published her steamy debut novel Masterson under a different title and pen name in August of 2015.

Thanks to strong reader support of her alpha male character, Roman Masterson, she was encouraged to continue with the series and published the entire Masterson Trilogy the following year. She hasn't looked back since and continues to write novels featuring strong alpha men and the smart women they seek to claim.

A romance junkie for sure, you can find Lisa watching a romantic comedy, reading a romance novel, or writing one of her own most days of the week. If she's not doing that, she's outside in the garden tending to her roses.

Lisa is the wife of one alpha (whom she met in college), mother to four girls, and two labradoodles. Get news on releases, sales and giveaways when you become one of Lisa's VIP readers at : http://LisaLangBlakeney.com/VIP